SPECIAL MESSAGE TO READERS

THE ULVERSCROFT FOUNDATION
(registered UK charity number 264873)
was established in 1972 to provide funds for
research, diagnosis and treatment of eye diseases.
Examples of major projects funded by
the Ulverscroft Foundation are:-

- The Children's Eye Unit at Moorfields Eye Hospital, London
- The Ulverscroft Children's Eye Unit at Great Ormond Street Hospital for Sick Children
- Funding research into eye diseases and treatment at the Department of Ophthalmology, University of Leicester
- The Ulverscroft Vision Research Group, Institute of Child Health
- Twin operating theatres at the Western Ophthalmic Hospital, London
- The Chair of Ophthalmology at the Royal Australian College of Ophthalmologists

You can help further the work of the Foundation
by making a donation or leaving a legacy.
Every contribution is gratefully received. If you
would like to help support the Foundation or
require further information, please contact:

THE ULVERSCROFT FOUNDATION
The Green, Bradgate Road, Anstey
Leicester LE7 7FU, England
Tel: (0116) 236 4325
website: www.foundation.ulverscroft.com

SEEING IS DECEIVING

When Vivian Seymour is found shot dead, inexperienced corporate attorney Gail Brevard is given the case. But she's up against her superiors, the Judge and the Prosecuting Attorney — no one wants her to win. A web of circumstantial evidence traps nineteen-year-old defendant Damon Powell, and he admits that on the evening in question he had the murder weapon. Gail believes in Damon's innocence, but with the judge continually ruling against her, how can she ever prove it?

LIONEL WEBB
with MARY W. BURGESS

---◆---

SEEING IS
DECEIVING

Complete and Unabridged

LINFORD
Leicester

First published in Great Britain

First Linford Edition
published 2013

Copyright © 2011 by Lionel Webb

British Library CIP Data

Webb, Lionel.
  Seeing is deceiving. - -
  (Linford mystery library)
  1. Detective and mystery stories.
  2. Large type books.
  I. Title II. Series
  823.9′2–dc23

  ISBN 978–1–4448–1439–2

Published by
F. A. Thorpe (Publishing)
Anstey, Leicestershire

Set by Words & Graphics Ltd.
Anstey, Leicestershire
Printed and bound in Great Britain by
T. J. International Ltd., Padstow, Cornwall

This book is printed on acid-free paper

1

Long before the sensational trial began, and long after it was over, the Cathcart locals lusted after every detail of the police's grisly discovery. Articles were written and television features were aired, and all those who were interviewed declared that it must have been 'just awful,' and they didn't know what they would have done if they had found something 'so terrible.' Internet chat groups were set up just so that people's opinions on every angle of the case could be exchanged.

The two police officers involved had taken no other important part in the case, beyond their court testimonies, but each responded differently when questions were posed to them. Charlie Hudson, the younger of the two, hoped he was on his way to bigger and better things on the force. He welcomed ~~any and~~ all interviews and tended to play up his role in the discovery, including the considerable pain he had endured as a result of his injury.

Jonas 'Wag' Waghorn (or 'Wag the Dog,' as he was known behind his back), the older partner, retired as quickly as he could after the trial. He consistently downplayed his part in the capture of the suspect and spoke as little as possible about the event and its aftermath. But he always insisted, when he couldn't avoid being questioned, that he was 'darn glad' he hadn't been more closely involved with the 'whole brutal, bloody mess.'

* * *

'Whoa! Just take it easy here, Charlie,' Jonas said to his partner who, as usual, was slouched behind the wheel of their patrol car. 'I want to live long enough to retire in a few months. Then I'm gonna take the missus to Fort Lauderdale, catch me some rays, and go to the races every day.'

Hudson sighed. He had heard all this before and was sick to death of the old geezer's ramblings. He made a quick right turn into a lush secluded enclave. 'Nothing much is gonna happen in Long Hills tonight, I wager,' he offered sullenly.

Wag merely yawned and nodded.

Long Hills was where the wealthier denizens of Cathcart holed up, like fat cats, in their expensive homes. Hudson, who was eager to make his mark in the community, always perked up a little when their rounds took them toward 'The Hills.'

'Slow down!' Jonas growled. 'Stretch things out a little, kid.'

Although it went against Hudson's instincts to dawdle, he admitted to himself that there was one advantage. Moving at a snail's pace, he'd be able to eyeball each and every property, and if he did see anything off-kilter, he might save a rich man's goods, or even a few lives, and thus receive a fat reward or commendation for his efforts. Charlie Hudson's brain was filled with all kinds of romantic, if unrealistic, notions about his role as a cop.

Just as he slowed down to the speed of a race walk, Wag made another request.

'Pull over there . . . into the side road.'

'Any reason for that?' Hudson asked, his hopes rising.

'I have to take a leak, if you wanna know. You get to my age and it's a holiday when you can hold it for five whole minutes.'

Hudson suspected that his partner would take longer than actually necessary. On one balmy summer's night recently he had caught the older man lying on the grass and 'resting his eyes,' while on one of these so-called 'nature calls.'

This November night, however, three weeks short of Thanksgiving, was chilly, and Waghorn came back to the car quick enough. He cursed the heater, blew into his hands, and commented resentfully that he had read, 'Just today,' that the temperature had reached seventy-five degrees in Fort Lauderdale. 'Can you imagine that? Well, let's take a sniff around,' he said finally, when Charlie made no response. 'But if you see anythin' goin' down that might be at all iffy, do me a favor — look the other way and save my pension.'

'All right, all right.' Hudson had learned the hard way that it was easier to say something non-committal than argue or try to tell Waghorn how outrageous his attitude was. He glanced out to his left, then suddenly slowed the car even further before stopping altogether.

'You want to grab some Z's, kid, that's OK by me, but pull into a side . . . '

'Shhh! Not so loud!'

When Waghorn looked out, his rheumy eyes following the younger man's silent hand signal, all he saw was one of the big houses, back off the side of the road, that looked like all the other big houses in this area. What he *didn't* see was anything that might have started the young cop's dandruff to itch.

'In front,' Hudson whispered urgently.

At first Waghorn thought he was looking at the shadow of some tree or bush, but then his ruddy face registered uncertainty.

'Somebody's out there looking up at the house, that's all,' he muttered.

'Stop breathin' in my ear!' Hudson growled.

'All right, somebody's out there. What about it? Probably walkin' the dog or somethin' . . . '

'I'm going to find out what he's doin' up there. It just don't look right to me.'

'All right . . . ' the older man relented. 'I'll come with you. But hold on a minute, I can't get my left foot out from under the seat here. Okay, got it now.'

Hudson led the way silently but quickly, with the more experienced Waghorn taking time to see if anyone else was near the road before he brought up the rear. The chill November air hit both men harshly, but Hudson, adrenaline running high, was less affected.

The intruder had just turned away from the house when Hudson called out, 'Hold it!'

The stranger whirled around, saw both of the cops for the first time and also noticed that Waghorn had stayed off to one side, blocking the quickest way out to the road.

'Who are you?' he asked uncertainly.

'Police,' Hudson snapped back, with authority. 'Who are *you*? And what are you up to here?'

'I live here,' the youth said. The rough voice ended in a frightened whine.

'You don't sound sure of it.'

'I'm not from around here, but I'm

staying with my . . . uncle.'

'Floyd Seymour? The builder? That's whose house you're hanging around.'

'Yeah, that's right. Floyd Seymour's my uncle.' A thin smile touched the corners of the young man's lips.

'Then maybe you won't mind,' Hudson said, 'if we go up there and check it out?'

'Do what you want.' The youth didn't budge.

'You're comin' with us,' Hudson said.

The lad's features grew even sharper as Hudson walked toward him.

'We're going to play 'sandwich,' kid,' Hudson said, as Waghorn drew up even with him. 'With you in the middle.'

Wag, who had been observing the young man closely, suddenly pointed. 'What's that stain on your clothes?'

The youth pretended to look down, but he was off and running hard before either cop could give chase. Hudson pounded after him, taking long, loping steps. Waghorn couldn't hope to match his younger partner's speed, but that was OK, the wily old veteran thought. It had crossed his mind that their quarry might

7

try doubling back to take the nearest path across the yard and out to the road and freedom.

Wag headed into a dense copse of trees, not sure where the clearing lay at either side, then stopped, blinking a little when the moonlight was suddenly obscured. He paused briefly to orient himself and the youth, who indeed had circled back, almost knocked him down, just about slamming the remaining breath out of his body. Stunned though he was, Wag managed to grab on to the young man's arm and hold tight.

Meanwhile, Charlie Hudson, huffing up from the other direction, suddenly lost his balance and yelled. He fell forward against the struggling youth, which, happily, allowed his partner to get an even firmer grip on the intruder's wiry arm.

Charlie gasped, 'I twisted my ankle. On some rock, I think.' He stared down at the ground furiously, and Waghorn had the weird notion that Hudson was going to kick the rock. But instead the younger officer exclaimed out loud, bent over, and came up with an object which he carried a few paces into the moonlight so he could examine it better, then limped back, ominously silent.

'Whatcher' got?' Waghorn queried.

'A gun, that's what!' Hudson grimaced through his discomfort. 'The kid was carrying!'

And before Waghorn could make any kind of response to this startling news, Hudson balled up a fist and hit the youth savagely in the midsection, causing the young man to double over with a gasp of pain.

'Don't try that again,' Waghorn said angrily to his partner,

'He deserved it,' Hudson said, his lips compressed thinly.

'You know what you are?' Wag said. 'You're a loose cannon, is what you are.'

'Him! It's all his fault.'

But the older cop was in no mood for an extended discussion. He made the decision to take control of the situation. 'Now, I ain't gonna leave you alone with him and you're not in any shape to move around, so *I'll* have to take him up to the Seymours and check out his story myself.'

'No. No. I'll go along,' Hudson grunted stubbornly. After all this trouble he was determined not to waste this golden opportunity to impress the Seymours with his bravery under fire.

'Move it, then,' Waghorn conceded. 'It's cold out here.'

After somewhat belatedly reading the intruder his rights, the two cops led their now-cuffed captive to the front steps of the Seymour house and paused. Waghorn didn't know one style of house from any other, but he knew it was the sort of place he would never be invited into. Hudson, shrugging through the pain of his possibly twisted ankle, hesitated as well.

'It doesn't look like anyone's home,' he said finally, deeply disappointed. 'I can make it up those stairs to the front entrance though and check. I'll do it somehow.'

'There might be some kinda basement entrance 'round t'other side,' Waghorn offered. 'Let's look . . . Wait, I think it's open! Look, the front door isn't even locked! Guess these rich buggers don't bother to lock their doors around here 'cause they think us cops'll protect 'em, but I don't like the looks of this . . . Too quiet by far . . . '

'We'd better go in anyway and check around,' Hudson muttered, 'just to make sure that the people are — you know, all right.'

'For once, you're on the money.' Waghorn led their little group up the steps and hesitated in the tiled foyer just inside the front door. He and Hudson still had their bit parts to play in the bloody tragedy about to unfold before them.

2

It had crossed Gail Brevard's mind more than once that morning that in the few weeks since she'd been away from the firm, everything might have changed. But of course she was wrong. The luxurious reception area was still deadly pristine — and quiet as a tomb, with one lone receptionist behind a counter, working away at her nails and occasionally answering one of the many phone lines arrayed in front of her. The back workrooms and law library, by contrast, were hubbubs of activity, with paralegals and interns jabbering away like magpies to one another, all complaining that the work of a law practice was never done by . . . 'lawyers.' She understood that they all played a role in the practice, and even had a good working relationship with most of them — but oh how she wished they didn't all behave as if they were the sole lifeblood of the firm.

Frank Kirshbaum, one of the young associates, stopped her in the hall and beamed happily at her. 'That Dollinger matter worked out pretty well for you, I hear.'

'Yes it did, Frank, thanks. It was a good settlement, and frankly they deserved to pay through the nose, after what they did to those people. Justice, you might say, has been served.'

'Well, there should be *some* compensation in law, aside from the money, I mean,' Frank said.

She smiled to herself. Frank was obviously envious that he hadn't been the one to handle the lucrative case, but at least he didn't allow his envy to rear its ugly head like some she knew. Good man. He might go far in the 'law biz,' as her ex-husband Lorne sometimes called it scornfully.

After exchanging a few more pleasantries with her colleagues, Gail was headed back to her own cubby-hole of an office when one of the secretaries waylaid her.

'The Judge asked to see you soon as you came in, Ms. Brevard.' There was

13

only one former judge in the firm of Maynard and Imlach.

'Tell him I'll be there just as soon as I put my things away.'

Her office had been vacuumed and dusted and her plants watered while she'd been in Cleveland, settling the hash of the infamous Dollinger family and their crusty old patriarch, but nothing else had changed. Except for the facsimiles of her diploma and law degree hanging on the wall, there wasn't one other unnecessary decoration in the room. As she stepped inside the door she noted with satisfaction how comfortable, yet impersonal, the room felt, which was just the way a law office ought to feel and look.

She took a moment to check her appearance in the closet mirror. A tall, slender redhead with attractive regular features gazed back at her. She had her makeup down to a minimum, highlighting her creamy complexion just enough to set off vivid green eyes. Her well-cut suit was softened today with a silky pale blouse and pearl ear studs. Her expensive leather walking pumps were her one concession to comfort. Gail was every bit as ambitious as the next person — perhaps even more so, as Lorne had complained bitterly in the heat of their gradually escalating arguments — but she had always refused to dress to make herself uncomfortable or edgy in any way. That would surely compromise the work, which was always her first priority.

She paused once more in the corridor to query a new recruit about a matter she knew he had been handling, and was told glumly that the verdict had gone against him. She touched his elbow to express sympathy, but didn't critique his efforts, let alone tell him that in her opinion the matter should have been handled differently in order to squeeze the opposite verdict out of the cantankerous jury.

'Come in, Gail — have a seat!' Judge Morin called out jovially as she knocked discreetly, then entered an office as different from hers as night from day. An artificial gas fireplace blazed cheerfully against the far wall, and every inch of the expensive wood paneling was crowded with one-of-a-kind artwork. A framed caricature of Morin that had appeared with a friendly article in the local *Sun* some years earlier held place of honor behind his polished mahogany desk. Family and political photos shared pride of place here and there, and numerous commemorative plaques, mementos from the Judge's travels, and other artifacts of interest were displayed on every sparkling flat surface available. A huge gray trilobite sat implacably in the middle of an antique Chinese red lacquered trunk. Gail gingerly deposited herself on one end of a black leather sofa and murmured a response to the Judge's greeting.

Behind his desk the distinguished judge reposed, his silver-rimmed glasses perched forward on his nose. His opponents in court often referred to him as the 'Silver Fox,' and he had the enviable reputation of being able to smile wholesomely at juries and set even the most unfriendly and uncooperative of witnesses at ease. As a judge he had made a point of never openly criticizing the lawyers appearing in front of him, and since entering private practice, he had more often than not ended up in the winning column. Judge Morin counted a large number of friends within Cathcart's legal community, but none of his colleagues relished appearing against him.

He stood up and courteously offered Gail tea or coffee from a well-stocked cart in the corner. That much settled, he congratulated her again on the happy outcome of the Dollinger affair and returned to his desk.

'I'm glad you took a few extra days off,' he said, sipping delicately at the herbal tea he had taken for himself. 'You stayed home for some of it, I suppose. How is your mother? Good. And how's your brother doing these days?'

'Erle is as well as can be expected,' she said, giving her unvarying response to that question.

'Poor boy. Well, who would have guessed that a son of Joe Norris's would be — well, I'm sorry, Gail. I didn't mean to bring up all that unhappiness, but you'll find as you become older you often replay every incident in your lifetime and mix 'em all together until they turn into a kind of poisoned stew, I suppose.'

She shrugged it off and changed the subject. 'Now that I'm all rested up, Judge, what's on the agenda?'

'I think you need something that'll take your mind off the Dollinger unpleasantness. You should be able to keep to your everyday schedule and take care of this new matter quite easily.'

'I'll be glad to fix a traffic ticket for you, Judge, if I possibly can,' she joked.

Morin gave a wan smile in response. 'Good to see you in such a happy mood, Gail. No, this is an entirely different case, of the sort you haven't dealt with before, and refreshing on that account alone.'

'Is there a case file to bring me up to speed?'

'No, mostly the newspaper accounts. You'll be starting with this matter from just about scratch.' Morin nudged his silver-tipped glasses briefly up off his nose, as if to show that this was, indeed, a 'really serious' matter. 'This is a capital case,' he added, a bit cautiously.

'A *criminal* case?' Gail stared at him in disbelief.

'Murder,' Randolph Morin intoned.

'And you want *me* to defend, sir? You know I've never had the slightest experience in a criminal case outside of law school.' She was stumbling over her words now, horrified at the implications before her.

'Well, you'll manage this one just fine, I'll warrant.'

'Judge, if I've been chosen to take on a murder case, handicapped with my inexperience, I'm inclined to believe that you *expect* me to lose.'

The 'Silver Fox' suddenly disappeared before her eyes. The cheerful countenance grew frosty, the jovial chin thrust itself out in belligerence — and every word of his reply was crafted to inspire acquiescence.

'Now you listen to me, Gail. If you don't care to take on this *pro bono* case for the good of the firm, then I really have no choice but to wish you a long, unchallenging career away from Morin and Imlach.'

Gail sat in stunned silence, his ugly words buzzing about in her brain like so many angry bees. She understood that whatever she said or did in the next few moments was key to her future. A wrong move here, and she'd forever lose any chance of continuing at Cathcart's most prestigious law firm, doing the work she loved best.

'Then I suppose I'd better get back to my office and wait for those papers,' she said, hoping she was making it clear that she had no desire to sever her connection with the firm. Yet she was just as determined not to apologize for her initial reluctance.

'Thank you, Gail,' Morin said. 'I knew you'd make the right decision.' The glasses slumped back down his nose again. He reclined back in his comfy leather swivel chair and took another swig of tea. If it was a battle of wills that had just ensued, there was no clear winner of the debate.

★　★　★

It crossed Gail's mind that Morin might not send the paperwork over, preferring to let her know indirectly that her services were no longer needed. She was just opening a desk drawer to get some idea of how much she'd have to cart home, when Morin's private secretary suddenly swung open the door and stepped in carrying a thin file which she plopped down on the corner of the desk. Gail closed the drawer and grabbed up the folder with relief.

'Hang on a minute, will you, Britney. I might have a few questions about this.' The file itself seemed to consist of little but newspaper stories. Brit, she knew, had an appetite for sensational news, and if this murder was a big one, she was certain to know all the current gossip about it. Gail was going to need every advantage she could muster.

'Sure, Gail, I don't have anything to do for about twenty minutes — but don't tell the judge that!' She winked conspiratorially.

Gail began perusing a newspaper article headlined 'Seymour Heiress Brutally Murdered.'

'Vivian Seymour? Somebody killed Floyd Seymour's daughter?'

'Haven't you heard about it? No one in town has talked about anything else since it happened.'

Gail was tempted to remind the secretary that she had been out of town for several weeks, but refrained from the obvious.

The details of the case became clear in the first couple of stories. A young man named Damon Powell had been picked up for loitering in front of the Seymour house late at night. Stupidly, he'd tried to throw away a gun, one that apparently had taken Vivian Seymour's life. Several bullets had been spent, doing what the *Sun* described as 'hideous damage.' Powell had been acquainted with the victim, and one of the last stories stated that it was known that he 'hated' her.

'According to this, the Powells have hired a lawyer to defend Damon.'

'They hired one of those street-type guys who wouldn't be allowed through the front door of *this* firm,' Britney said disdainfully. 'Some fellow named Watson, I think.'

Gail had heard of Watson (although she

couldn't think of his first name at the moment), and knew he had a reputation for being very good at his specialty.

'Damon's mother insisted on hiring somebody else, but that doesn't necessarily mean the case isn't *pro bono*.'

Gail supposed the Powells were looking for a more prestigious firm to defend 'Sonny Boy,' which was just plain stupid, since Watson, experienced as he was in criminal matters, could have managed a much better defense for the kid.

The next article was headlined '*State Will Consider Death Penalty in Powell Case*.' She shook her head furiously. She was more than willing to put herself forward, but she would hate to proceed if she was convinced her clumsiness could result in a possible execution. In that instance it would make no difference at all if it cost her the valuable connection with Morin and Imlach. She refused to risk gambling away someone's life for the job.

She tucked the clipping back in the file and pulled out the next one in order. The headline shouted: '*Special Prosecutor*

Appointed in Powell Case.' A separate box printed in italics added: 'To Ask for the Death Penalty.' A photograph of the Special Prosecutor was included. Gail took one look and her usually pleasant features hardened.

'Put through a call for me,' she said to Britney, who had begun looking anxiously at her watch. She handed the clipping across. 'Get me an appointment with Turner Redland. Immediately.'

'When will you be free to see him?'

'This very moment is none too soon for me,' Gail growled, a frown wrinkling her brow. 'I'm looking forward to it.'

⋆　⋆　⋆

'Gail!' Turner greeted her, opening the door to his office. 'This is a pleasant surprise.'

He led her to the visitor's chair and helped her to her seat.

'You're looking great.'

'Thanks.' She didn't bother to return the compliment. He must know, even after the years that had passed, that he was still a good-looking man, with that lion-like head and those piercing eyes, but she could almost predict how mercilessly the years to come would change him by weakening those eyes, coarsening his skin, and destroying his physique. He might still be a ladies' man, but the prime time in everyone's life was only a certain decade or so, and Turner was on a fast track to the other side.

'Are you practicing law these days?' he asked.

'I'm with Morin and Imlach,' she said quietly. Had he not known even *that* much about her?

'A good group.' He beamed at her like a favorite uncle. 'They can take the rough edges off any of our brethren.'

'I know that.'

She didn't have to ask about him, having seen his name again and again in the news as he had climbed the ladder, making his reputation in the state capitol, appearing in gang prosecutions and disposing of high-profile drug cases. It wasn't surprising that Turner had been appointed Special Prosecutor in this case, which was sure to make waves around the state wherever the movers and shakers gathered.

'I don't see a ring on your finger, Gail. Are you and Lorne separated?'

'We're divorced.'

He turned those dynamite eyes on her full bore, and she knew that he was speculating if there was still some chance he could get together with her again. She was too cynical to suppose he was particularly fond of her at this point. Ambition had been as large a part of her life as of his own. But she also knew he wasn't one to miss out on having a fling, just so long as it was clearly understood that marriage wasn't in the cards.

Today she made it crystal clear that she was there for business purposes only, and she definitely wasn't interested in opening up any old wounds. Still, she couldn't help remembering the young Turner Redland, the most promising of her law school colleagues. It had seemed natural at the time that the two of them would become an item. But what had surprised her most was that they turned out to have much more in common than she'd thought initially. Turner, like Gail, was a hard worker who didn't need to rely on his natural charm to get ahead. More importantly, he had made time to study intensely, and even to mentor those students who would never be in his league.

They had had so much in common, in fact, that Gail was bound to get the idea that they ought to get married and become law partners as well, and eventually she summoned the courage to bring up the topic.

'We'd be good in business together,' she pointed out.

'I've thought about that too,' he admitted.

Not comfortable in hiding her feelings from him, she added, 'We could both do worse than get married and form a real partnership.'

'*You* could do worse, don't you mean?'

He had spoken so promptly that it was obvious he had already thought this through — and that was what Gail could never forgive. If only he'd taken a minute before answering, it would have let her down easier, and she wouldn't have held such a grudge all these years. But just as soon as those words tumbled out so awkwardly from her lips, Turner turned into a stranger — someone she didn't know — and didn't want to know.

'Suppose we got married and suppose we had a kid,' he said coldly. 'Do you *really* think I'd take the risk that my child might not turn out all right, might be like your brother?'

She had held her tongue, instead of responding angrily, willing herself not to burst into the bitter tears welling up inside her.

'And to tell you the truth, Gail,' he went on, seemingly oblivious to her pain, 'I don't think you'll ever find a guy willing to take a chance like that. There are plenty of women out there with normal backgrounds . . .'

And then, having damaged her beyond repair, he smiled brightly and concluded, 'I really didn't want to hurt your feelings, but you see how it is . . .'

From then on Gail had avoided Turner like the plague and just got on with her studies. A few years after she had passed the bar, she met Lorne Brevard, a personable young attorney, whose practice seemed inexplicably unsuccessful. When he'd proposed she'd agreed readily, certain that between her brisk energy and his charming personality, they could turn his limping business around.

All of which would have been great, if only the marriage had worked out. She did well in their small practice, outperforming an increasingly perplexed Lorne, who finally broke the news to her that he had decided to take a salaried job with the city. There he wouldn't have to worry about bills to pay, caseloads to juggle, or clients' hands to hold. Left unsaid was the more important fact — that he would no longer have to compete with her.

If they had been more compatible, she would have loyally stood by a husband who was content to be nothing more than a minor civil service employee. But eventually, she realized she just couldn't live the lie any more — and she became convinced that the dead-end situation was affecting her work. Her divorce was uncontested and granted forthwith.

In the meantime, Gail's mother, who had known Randolph Morin from the old days, when Gail's father was still alive and practicing estate law, had asked him to consider her bright young daughter for his firm. The ex-judge promised he would do what he could for her, and he'd been as good as his word. The rest, as they say, had been history.

★ ★ ★

She wasn't surprised that Turner didn't seem to have the slightest interest in what had happened to her while he'd been out making a name for himself.

'Well, Counselor,' he said, as he took his seat behind an oversized desk piled high with pending files and paperwork, 'What can you do for me?'

'I can keep you from making a fool of yourself in court.'

'What do you mean?'

'I'm taking on the defense in the Damon Powell case.'

'Are you now? And how do you

propose to do that?'

'You'll find out if we discuss the case like sensible adults.'

'What angles of the Powell case do you want to talk about, Gail?'

'Your request for the death penalty will do for a start.'

'Don't preach to me about the death penalty being such an 'abomination,' Gail. How about the crime that has been committed? These are individuals who can't be saved. These are creatures against whom we must protect ourselves.' He sounded as if he was making a political speech. 'Citizens who are afraid to take on the responsibility of imposing the death penalty take the risk that one day these beasts will be free to strike again.'

'And if the wrong person is executed in error,' she said, 'what then? What does society say about *that* miscarriage of justice?'

'To begin with, this case has been double-checked so often that you can be certain there's an extremely strong likelihood that the real culprit is already in the dock.'

'But suppose that that 'once-in-a-lifetime'

error does occur and the wrong person is executed, Turner. You can't take it back!'

'The scientific evidence is much more accurate now than it was, even five years ago. And if you made the effort to delve into the subject, you'd be aware of that fact.'

'But *if* the wrong person *was* executed, Turner? Where's all your fine 'scientific evidence' then?'

'Who's to say such an execution, even in the event of an error, might not be a deterrent to some other criminal bent on murder? Wouldn't that go a long way towards keeping the crime rate down?'

'Yes. A great lesson for us all,' she muttered.

'A lot of life is ugly, Gail, as I'm sure you're aware.'

'It's useful to think that way if you're a Special Prosecutor with plans to run for high office — .'

'Bad jokes to one side, Gail, is there anything else you wanted to talk about?'

'The evidence against this boy.'

'He's *not* a boy. Nineteen is old enough to stand trial for murder. And the blood on his clothing is evidence. The gun dropped by his side is evidence. Being found loitering outside the house where the murder was committed is evidence. It's not just a series of unconnected complaints against a young man with no record. He's not being 'picked on' with nothing but circumstantial evidence to go by. And we can also show that he had been in contact with the victim, that he knew her.'

'So much for opportunity — but what about motive?'

'We come up a little short on motive, I'll grant you that much.' Turner warmed to his subject once more. 'But a real motive can be so trivial that it could be missed or ignored or deemed not believable — and it must be framed in concepts that other people will agree with. In all fairness, Gail, this isn't a TV show — *life* isn't a TV show, and you know that as well as anyone.'

Not only did she grudgingly agree with him, but it had already crossed her mind that his ideas on the subject of motive were something she'd be able to turn on end — to use during the trial, perhaps during some speech to the jury or an off-hand remark. Turner and his preconceived beliefs might be more helpful to her than he realized.

'I can see that we aren't going to get much further.' She stood and he followed suit. 'Turner, do you remember *The People vs. Barber*?'

'Refresh my memory.'

'You appeared for the People and I stood up for the defendant.'

'You and me on the same case?' She didn't know why she should be surprised that he remembered so little about their shared past. 'I swear I don't recall anything like that, especially not a capital case, Gail.'

'It was a practice case we tried in law school.'

'Oh, one of *those*.' He dismissed the topic as he opened the door for her. She wouldn't have been at all surprised to see him follow up with a formal bow, if he thought it would antagonize her even further.

'That case — the case that we tried,

Turner, under conditions that duplicated an actual trial as much as possible — I beat you — and I'll do it again this time.'

She turned away leaving him open-mouthed; and, head high, she strode out of his office.

* * *

A visit to Damon Powell was next on Gail's agenda, and she intended to outline both the advantages and the drawbacks to entering a plea of guilty of second degree murder or manslaughter, as opposed to a plea of not guilty of murder one. Turner might be inclined to refuse such a deal at the outset, but she felt sure she could argue him around to it.

On the other hand, she suspected that Damon Powell's parents would likely turn down any deal that would require an admission of guilt.

Assuming then that there would be a major trial, Gail was determined to beat Turner at his own game, and to fling their so-called 'expertise' into the collective faces of the good citizens of Cathcart.

Nor would it bother her much to see the astonished look on Randolph Morin's face when a novice at criminal law won out. Gail's competitive instincts had been tweaked — and that always caused her to come out swinging.

*   *   *

Congestion forced her to park in a lot some distance from the main entrance to the Cathcart Detention Center. The dank gray building looked as though it had been standing there grimly since the soot-soaked days of Charles Dickens. Pale sunlight with no warmth peeked through the chilly afternoon sky, making the complex feel even more forbidding, and Gail tugged her heavy coat around her tightly as she scurried for the steps.

The anteroom was high-ceilinged and drafty, and smelled like a chlorinated indoor pool. A burly sergeant was perched on duty at a desk in the northeast corner, and he looked up curiously at the sight of her.

'I'm Counsel, here to see Damon

Powell,' she explained.

'Oh yeah, you're the lady lawyer, ain'tcha? Wait here a minute. Somebody'll come escort you over to the 'royal suite.''

Soon a door swung open in the farthest wall, and an officer poked his head out and nodded at her.

'I'm Rolfe,' he said. 'You must be Powell's lawyer. You got any ID?'

She showed him her legal ID card together with a directive from Turner on his office stationery.

'That's it,' Rolfe said, making his decision after reading no more than a few words. 'That's all I need . . . come along, please.'

He led the way up a stairwell as gray as the outside of the building. ('The elevators are all on the blink right now,' he said by way of explanation.) This facility was mostly used to house the drunk and disorderly and low-level misdemeanor cases. People accused of major crimes were transported to the larger, more comfortable quarters located near the courthouse. However, an exception to the norm had been made in the case of Damon Powell.

Gail distracted herself from the unpleasant thought that the overpowering odor of chlorine and sweat might permeate her clothing and never leave. 'You think he's guilty?' she asked her guide, as they made their way up the concrete stairs, their footsteps echoing hollowly behind them.

Rolfe nodded. 'Sure I think he's guilty. I'm appalled that anyone would offer to stick up for him in court.'

'But how do you know he's guilty before he's even been tried? How can you be so sure?'

'Because I'm a cop, ma'am, and believe me, cops *always* know.'

Gail didn't bother to respond, since they had reached the landing at the top of the stairs. Rolfe, huffing a bit from his exertions, turned abruptly and led her into a small, over-heated cell furnished sparsely with chairs placed on either side of a plain table running the width of the room. A heavy-duty screen mesh separated the table down the middle, and initials and graffiti had been gouged into the wood on the opposite side. Rolfe turned his back on her and marched out of the room.

A door on the opposite side of the room swung open and a different uniformed handler motioned to a slender young man slouching behind him, whose shadowed face she wasn't quite able to see.

The jailer snarled, 'Ya wanna scoot out afore yer ten minutes is up, lady, jes' punch that buzzer there on yer left.'

'Thanks,' she replied coolly, 'I will if necessary.'

3

Damon Powell broke into a whining rant, even before his guard could get the door slammed shut and latched behind him.

'So you're my new mouthpiece? *Everyone* is tryin' to get me buried and I wanna know what *you're* planning to do to help 'em.'

It was a challenge, Gail knew, that had better be answered immediately — and in no uncertain terms.

'Well, *I* can see how *you're* going to help them do just that,' she retorted, 'and I can hear it in the disrespectful tone of your voice, too.'

One look at him and any jury would declare him guilty on the spot, without even listening to the evidence. Damon's hair was long and straggly, and looked none too clean. He lounged back in his chair, his eyes hidden by dark glasses.

'Take those shades off, for a start,' Gail said.

'Wha'?'

'You heard me. I want to see your eyes when I'm talking to you.'

'My eyes are light green, so now you know.'

'Take those things off!' Gail ordered more vehemently.

Damon pursed his lips and looked around him, considering his options, then shrugged and laid the glasses on the table.

Gail said, 'I get the impression that you might be teachable.'

'And I get the impression I need a new mouthpiece.'

'What I am by profession is a lawyer.' She spoke firmly. 'You can call me Ms. Brevard or Counselor — that's all.'

'All right, all right, Counselor. Friends forever?' Damon mumbled sarcastically.

Gail found herself slightly amused by this difficult client. She wondered if he was testing her to see if he could get her to smile, or possibly change the mood of this meeting.

'Hear me out, then we'll have more time to talk about your case,' Gail put in before he could test her again. 'You can't wear long hair when you go into court, nor dark glasses. The people on your jury, and the judge himself, are likely to be conservative types who are appalled by anything that is different from the way it was when they were young.'

Damon nodded sullenly, but said nothing.

'Do you use drugs?'

'I've tried them a few times.'

'Marijuana? Anything harder?'

'A few lines of cocaine, sure, but never heroin.'

'Have you ever been arrested on a drug charge?'

'No arrests at all. I've got a clean sheet.'

'I hope you're not lying.'

He shrugged irritably. 'I can't convince *nobody* I'm innocent, so it's no surprise I can't convince *you*.'

'And while I think of it, you should try to cut out any slang or profanity when you talk to reporters or in court. You don't want to sound like a young hood. Do you understand?'

Another sullen nod. 'When are we

gonna talk about what happened?'

'We'll do it now if you want — but please don't come off like a thug.'

'Okay, ask me.'

'What on earth were you doing in Long Hills on the night Vivian Seymour was killed?'

'I was takin' a walk and that's all.'

'Do you walk there often? Alone and at night?'

'I've done it a few times. Even the cops can't make somethin' out of just takin' a walk.'

'And you swear you never entered the Seymour house before then? Is that what you're telling me?'

'I never went near the place — '

'All right, the police picked you up outside the house. What happened then?'

'The younger guy busted me and then the two of 'em dragged me into the house. The girl was already dead.'

After a few more questions about the circumstances of his arrest, Gail came to the most important point of her visit.

'On the night of November fifth, did you kill Vivian Seymour?'

'No!' Damon almost shouted. 'I swear I didn't touch that girl!'

Gail paused, going over the notes she had taken, and gathering her thoughts. 'Thank you, Damon, for answering my questions so willingly. But I must tell you that, without further proof or witnesses coming forward, you haven't got a prayer of convincing anyone, let alone a jury, that you're innocent. I also must tell you that, in my opinion, your best bet would be to plead guilty to some sort of a lesser charge. That means about ten to twenty years inside, less good behavior, of course.'

Damon took the news quietly, taking a moment to respond. 'My mother would come unglued,' he said finally, 'if I went before a judge and claimed I had done anything that horrible. Nope, I won't do it.'

'In other words, you're ready to battle for your life before a jury in court.' She had to admit to herself that it was the answer she was leaning toward as well.

'I guess you've got to find some other way to make my case,' he smiled.

'Well, if I can't, you'll be in jail for a very long time, if you don't draw a lethal injection, that is.'

'You gotta try, though.' He looked down at the table and looped his fingers around the stems of his dark glasses. 'If I don't get off, I'll never be with *her* again, and I couldn't take it, being without — never mind! Never mind none o' that! It's none o' your business, anyway.'

Obviously, there was some girl out there. Someone who Damon felt sure was on his side. And from the tone of his voice and the sudden fierce look that had crossed his face before he put those glasses back on, he had shut Gail out of the equation. For the sake of this unknown girl, and for the feelings he felt they shared, he would not plead guilty. It was almost enough to make Gail feel sorry for him, for the girl, and for herself, too, for that matter. And the very worse part of it was that his feelings for this unknown girl might have gained sympathy with the public — if he would allow her to bring it out.

'I can put private detectives to work on

this,' she said, as she gathered her briefcase and coat. 'Is there any chance they'll come up with information you *don't* want them to find? Now is the time to tell me. It won't go any further.'

'They might come up with the real killer — and get me outta this place,' he muttered.

For just a moment she resented him, not only for his youth and cluelessness, but because, unlike her poor brother, he was mentally intact. No, he didn't have a clue how fortunate he really was, even under these sad circumstances. She forced a trace of a smile to her lips as she told herself sternly not to be such a fool.

'So long,' he sang out as Gail rose, adding sassily, 'See ya in court.'

* * *

A middle-aged couple perched uncomfortably on a wooden bench in the anteroom as Gail was escorted back to the front of the facility. The man's eyes were shut, as if he was resting, or, perhaps in pain, but the woman looked as if her eyes were never closed. She was heavy, in both body and demeanor. In the chill air she clutched about her a beige coat with *faux* fur trim. Beneath the floppy lapels peaked a vivid red dress that couldn't have been more inappropriate for the place and circumstances.

'Miss Brevard?' she demanded in a deep throaty drawl, redolent of too many cigarettes. 'I'm Damon's mother.'

Gail smiled and approached the pair. As she neared them, Mr. Powell opened his pale eyes and rose to greet her. His gray face and even grayer thinning hair matched the equally gray slacks and sport jacket he had donned for this occasion.

'Well,' the woman began, 'You look a lot more respectable than that lawyer — Watson, whatever his name is — who was suggested to us first.'

'Thank you,' she said, suddenly remembering that Watson's first name was Hal. She hadn't been any more impressed by his appearance than Mrs. Powell, but she knew he had won a large number of criminal cases.

'And I want you to know,' Mrs. Powell

went on, 'that my son is *completely innocent* of all those terrible charges drummed up against him.'

Damon was right about one thing, Gail realized. A woman as strong-minded as this one would never agree to a guilty plea from her son in court. Such a plan was entirely out of the question.

'I asked Damon point blank if he did that terrible thing,' Damon's mother added insistently, 'and he swore he didn't. My son wouldn't lie to me. Never! Not even when he was no bigger than a finger did he ever lie to me!' Her voice had risen slightly, and ended on an unattractive screech.

There must be a primal maternal instinct which caused mothers to sound and act so much alike, Gail told herself, without considering how she herself might respond, if she ever became a member of that sorority.

Mr. Powell interrupted tactfully, 'We want to help, of course, in any way we can.'

'Do either of you have any idea who might have been involved?'

'Nobody,' Mrs. Powell said icily. 'Damon doesn't hang out with that sort . . .'

'Well, is there anyone else you can think of who might have more information about him?'

'More than me and Mr. Powell? Don't you believe it!'

'Is he seeing some girl steadily?' Gail pursued.

'Absolutely not! I won't allow him to get mixed up with just any girl, not until he's ready to make a living and support a family. Most of these girls just want to drag a decent young man down and keep him from bettering himself, just so they can buy things for themselves and have it easy, if you know what I mean.'

Gail certainly did know what she meant, but did Damon buy into his mother's attitude, her contempt for the young women of his acquaintance? With at least one girl, that didn't seem to be the case.

'Mrs. Powell, is there anything else helpful that you can tell me at this time?'

'Only that my son is innocent.' The older woman's eyes suddenly narrowed suspiciously. 'You don't sound like you believe that my boy's innocent. If that's true, then I want you off my boy's case as soon as possible.'

Mr. Powell intervened once more, trying to cover up his wife's rudeness. 'I'm certain that Miss Brevard will do the best job that's possible.'

His wife brushed those words aside with a meaty hand.

'Now, I've got some friends who are lawyers, men whose names you'd recognize at Morin and Imlach. And I must tell you that I intend to ask these friends of mine if they approve of the way you're handling Damon's case.'

'Do that, by all means.' And Gail turned away without another word and started for the door.

★　★　★

A shower back at her town house didn't entirely restore her spirits, but there were a few legal tasks she needed to attend to before she could even begin to consider any relaxation tonight.

She dialed the firm's investigative standby, the Goldthwaite Detective Agency. Old Hugo, the founder, wasn't in. But Hugo, Jr. was available, which suited her needs even better. The Goldthwaites did whatever the Cathcart citizenry required of them, that is, those who could afford their somewhat padded fees. The Goldthwaites had a reputation for delivering the goods, and they certainly knew where all the bodies in town were buried.

'Hugo, Gail Brevard here. I suppose you've heard that I'm defending in this Powell matter.'

'Sure have,' young Hugo said. 'We were a little shocked that that particular mess had been dropped into your lap.'

'Well, it has. If you'd rather not get involved, you'd better speak now or forever hold your peace.'

'Dad mentioned something about it to me just as soon as the story broke. We both agreed that if you asked for us, I'd be happy to take it on. Morin and Imlach are good clients of ours, so we want to keep 'em happy.'

'To start with, I want you to find out

everything you can about Damon Powell and his parents. *Everything*, from the year one up to day before yesterday.'

'Turner probably has someone on all that already.'

'All the same, I want a look at the dirt before Turner empties the vacuum cleaner.'

'How far do we go on the expenses?'

'Get the information first, and then we'll talk money. Don't worry about it.'

Even as she hung up, Gail was certain that there'd be a near-endless delay getting the expenses reimbursed by the Court. But if the Goldthwaites could come up with the sort of information she needed, she was willing to pay them out of her own pocket, if necessary.

4

The next Sunday dawned chilly, and although she would much rather have puttered around on her own, reviewing her notes on the Powell case, she'd promised to play hostess to her mother and brother for the afternoon. It would at least keep her mind off her first criminal appearance the next day. Her secret weapon was a nearby family-style restaurant that delivered, and if Mother had figured out that particular ploy, she chose to smile and compliment Gail's perfect table setting and made over the dishes, for which Gail was grateful.

Mother did launch her usual discussion about Gail's career, which was probably why she had come in spite of the unpleasant weather.

'Your Father would *never* have agreed to take on such a notorious case,' offered Mrs. Norris, tossing her expertly-coifed head. '*He* knew what it meant to be a corporate lawyer.'

Joseph Norris, Gail reflected cynically, would probably have defended Hitler if his firm had ordered him to — and Mother was well aware of it. But Alberta Norris couldn't resist the temptation of making her daughter squirm.

Gail didn't answer her mother, but instead turned to her brother Erle, with her usual instructions on how to manipulate the tablespoon without dribbling hot soup down his front. His face was smooth, with no worry lines to disrupt his bland features. Once again it crossed Gail's mind that Damon Powell, who was so much younger in real time, was so much older in every other way.

Erle suddenly pulled back and put both hands on the table. 'I have to go and use the pishy-button,' he announced in the deep voice that was always so disconcerting.

'It's over there,' Gail said, pointing to the hallway. 'The closest door.' She had given him exactly the same directions at least once, every time he visited.

Erle hesitated, then thrust out a hand

toward his sister. 'Show me. Please.'

Gail led him to the hallway where he leaned toward her to whisper, but Mother raised her voice to tell him to 'Be careful with Gail's things,' and he said nothing, but continued on into the bathroom.

Gail still was shaking her head to herself when she came back to hear Mother hammering on in full-throated rhetoric.

' . . . and you mustn't let that useless case take too long, dear. You simply can't spare the time away from your *real* practice.'

'I'll do what I can about that, Mother.' It was better not to argue.

'Personally, I think you're applying yourself so vigorously because you want to get the better of that boyfriend you had in college, the one who was appointed Special Prosecutor for this case. You know, Turner. More like stomach-turner, if you ask me! Smooth as butter, but a sneak all the same. Turn your back on him at your own risk, my dear.'

'I know.' It was surprising to Gail that Mother remembered anything at all except her own grievances, including her socially proper marriage to a man who had disappointed her by giving her a son who was retarded.

They heard Erle open the bathroom door, causing Mother to ask loudly, 'Did you flush?'

'Yes, Mama,' the disconcerting booming man's voice answered. 'Gail, will you come lead me back? I don't know the way.'

Gail had surmised that Erle wanted to ask her something Mother wasn't supposed to know about. She quickly scraped back her chair and headed for the dimly-lit corridor, but Mother, her lips compressed in disapproval, cut Gail off. 'I'll bring him back.'

Erle was escorted back with no more fuss and resumed his seat at the table, dealing somehow with his soup, until Gail took up the troublesome spoon and helped him finish. As she brought out the main dishes, Mother cut his meat and steamed carrots into tiny bits.

Mother waited until Erle was happily playing with the carrots before she rose, saying, 'Be right back,' and headed down the hallway herself.

Erle looked as if he couldn't believe his luck when Mother started to the bathroom. The door closed behind her and was followed by an immediate click of the lock. He leaned in Gail's direction and whispered what he had been waiting to ask all day: 'Can you loan me a penny?'

'Sure I can,' Gail whispered back, reaching for her nearby purse and tucking the coin into her brother's eager hand. 'Don't tell anyone about this. It'll be our secret.'

'No, I won't,' Erle agreed happily. 'Promise.'

Gail was able to keep on eating her meal. After all this time, all the disappointments, all the moments of hope that faded, the bitterness that had to be shunted aside, she was beyond anguish for him, beyond tears for the both of them.

★   ★   ★

Gail never felt nervous before an actual appearance in court, and today she was

57

looking forward to the anticipated joust against her opposition, unwilling to give him even the slightest advantage. She felt no difference between this preliminary motion than she did about any other she'd ever handled, as she hurried into the airy courtroom and took her place at the defendant's table.

Damon was led in to take the chair next to her. He wore a conservative navy blue suit, pale button-down shirt, and a subdued tie, all of which Gail had had delivered to him the night before at the jail. His black shoes were shined to a high gloss, and miracle of miracles, he sported a trim new hair cut.

'Do I look okay?' he asked nervously.

'You'll do,' Gail said. 'But you'll look even better if you can make the supreme sacrifice and not slouch in your chair.'

Thanks to Hugo, she now knew a lot more about Damon's personal life than at their first meeting, but none of it was all that helpful. He had kept out of the hands of the law for most of his nineteen years, but he hadn't done anything else worth a mention. He had drifted through school, even managing one year of junior college, had been in and out of jobs, dated a lot of different girls, and had a few fights. Just an average kid, except that he seemed less ambitious than most.

The fact of the matter was that Gail didn't feel the slightest tug of sympathy for him, beyond his present predicament. On the plus side, his ticket was cleaner than she would have expected.

A tall, heavy-set man nodded to her from the other table. 'I'm Richard Yeltoon,' he said, when Gail turned slightly in her chair to face him. 'I'm appearing for the People today.'

'Where's Turner?'

'Sitting this one out. Probably tied up with some legal group, if you want my guess.' He grinned.

Gail didn't respond. She had intended to do some fishing in prosecution waters by making a motion that would force Turner to put at least part of his case against Damon on the record. But without his presence, the associate could claim he didn't have the information, and Gail would more than likely leave the session empty-handed.

The judge emerged from a side door and seated himself in a comfortable leather chair behind the bench.

'Hear ye, hear ye,' the bailiff intoned. 'All persons having business with the Criminal Court of Cathcart, First District, Mr. Justice Passy presiding, draw near, give your attention, and ye shall be heard.'

The judge, a small, thin man, was sitting in for Judge West today. He glanced at Gail, then over her head at the onlookers.

'Let me take this opportunity to remind you that this is a capital case in which a motion will be heard shortly. I want no unseemly displays of laughter, approval, or disapproval from the spectators. Anyone violating my rules will be asked to leave. Remember this isn't *Court TV* here.'

There was a discrete murmuring from the crowd.

Damon muttered, 'My life is on the line and that idiot is telling jokes!'

Gail felt pretty much the same way, but

issued another reminder. 'Watch yourself, Damon! And straighten up, while you're at it.'

He glared at her, but obeyed.

The judge picked up a paper. 'This is the Defendant's motion for bail. The Defense is not putting on any witnesses today, I assume?'

'No, I have no witnesses, Your Honor,' Gail said. 'The burden of proof is not on the Defense.'

'I see that the Special Prosecutor hasn't chosen to favor us with his presence for the hearing of this motion.'

'Mr. Redland sends his profound apologies, but he was detained elsewhere by other pressing matters,' Yeltoon said.

'Mr. Redland's apologies are accepted — with prejudice. I take it that you have at least one witness to put on?'

'Yes, Your Honor.'

'Proceed.'

'The People call Dr. Anthony Colbert to the stand.'

A clerk walked out into the anteroom, calling the witness's name and returned with a tall, carefully groomed man who smiled warmly at the judge before being sworn in and seated in the witness box.

Yeltoon laid a half dozen pieces of paper down on the lighted lectern in front of the witness chair.

'For the record, Dr. Colbert, I have to ask about your qualifications.'

'I've been in psychiatric practice in Cathcart for fifteen years come February. And as for my degrees . . . ,' He sounded bored. It was obvious that the same words had come out of his mouth many times. The audience began to stir restlessly, having expected more fireworks and drama.

Gail broke in. 'The Defense will stipulate that Dr. Colbert is qualified as an expert witness.'

'Thank you,' said Yeltoon.

Damon muttered, 'What are you doing? Are you just going to let him crucify me without putting up any fight at all?'

'I'm choosing my battles, Damon. I'll have plenty of trouble with Yeltoon, or the judge, down the road, so why argue over this guy's qualifications?'

Yeltoon began again. 'Dr. Colbert, when did you see the defendant for the first time?'

'On the night of November fifth of this year, shortly after he had been detained by the police.'

'And where did you see him?'

'At police headquarters.'

'And what was his mood, in general?'

'He was upset — cursing and shouting. He made vague threats and it was necessary to 'talk him down.''

'Did you form any professional opinion about the defendant at that time?'

'No, since I didn't conduct any in-depth examination of him.'

'But did you feel that he might be a menace to the community if he were to be set free?'

Gail began to rise for an objection, but the judge interrupted irritably, 'There's no jury to impress here, Counselor, so rephrase your questions in a more straightforward way.'

'I beg the Court's pardon,' Yeltoon said. 'Now, Dr. Colbert, I've been hoping not to keep you too long as I realize that you have a busy practice to service.' Gail rolled her eyes. 'Can you tell us whether, in your opinion as a qualified psychiatrist, you feel that bail should be granted in this case?'

'I can't offer an opinion at this time, Mr. Yeltoon, for the reason I just gave, but I feel that there *may* be a potential for the defendant to do some harm to himself or others if he is freed on bail at this time.'

'Thank you, Doctor.' Yeltoon gathered his notes from the lectern with a flourish and bowed in Gail's direction. 'Yours.'

'Thank you. I wonder, Doctor, if you could tell the Court, in your *professional opinion*, just how many dangerous people there are walking around Cathcart these days?'

'I can't have any accurate idea how many there might be.'

'And yet, day follows day without most of those 'dangerous' people exploding or causing havoc. Do you suppose, in spite of that fact, that they should all be restrained or arrested?'

'In an ideal world, certainly.'

'But we don't live in an ideal world, do

we? And it might well be that the laws of our country protect the rights of some of those people you feel are so dangerous to themselves or others.'

There was a whisper of laughter from the onlookers.

The judge, looking even more irritable, said, 'Can you get on with it, Counselor? *If you please!*'

'I am attempting to show a bias on the part of this witness, Your Honor.'

'Take another tack, Counselor.'

'Very well, Your Honor. You told the Court that you've been in practice here for almost fifteen years,' she resumed. 'For how many of those years, Doctor, have you worked closely with the police and the District Attorney's office?'

'Nearly all of that time.' Colbert had been through this sort of questioning many times in the past. 'I've testified in two hundred fifty cases as a matter of fact.'

'Exactly that number?'

'I looked it up before coming here,' he smiled smugly. 'I knew I'd be asked.'

Gail proceeded as if she had expected

that answer. 'And in how many of those cases have you testified for the prosecution?'

'All but nine.'

'And in those nine cases, were you paid by the State for your services?'

'In two of those cases the clients were indigent, but I felt strongly enough about their innocence to testify without a fee, or *pro bono,* as it's called.' He turned to the jury with a self-satisfied smile.

Gail realized she'd given him too much latitude and went on the attack more directly. 'I'm happy to hear that you've seen fit to use your conscience in at least two cases out of so . . . '

The judge interrupted. 'Young woman — Counselor — apologies to the witness are in order.'

'Yes, Your Honor. I apologize to the Court and to Dr. Colbert for having engaged in personalities. May I now resume my cross-examination?'

'Proceed.'

'Dr. Colbert, when were you called by the police to examine the defendant . . . at what time, precisely?'

'It must have been a little after midnight.'

'So you were available to the police at that unlikely time of night?'

'Actually, I was, yes, just as the police themselves are required to make themselves available at all hours. It comes with the job.'

'I see. Your job working for the police of Cathcart.' She hurried on ignoring the threatening glower from the judge. 'Now, exactly how much time did you spend with the defendant that night — do you think? Do you have any idea?'

'I'd say about sixty minutes or so. Yes, I believe I was with him for approximately one hour.'

'And during that time were you ever left alone with him?'

'No, never.'

'So, one or more policemen or District Attorney's representatives were always in the room with the two of you?'

'During that hour I was in the defendant's company, yes. We were never left alone together.'

'During that period of time, the time

you were in the defendant's company, but under supervision by one or two other officers, did he ever threaten any violence to you or any of the others?'

'He *threatened* it, in so many words, yes.'

'But did he actually attack you or anyone else? Did he *do* anything other than verbally threaten you? Was any attempt made by the defendant to harm you physically in any way?'

'Since there were always other people in the room, of course he knew he couldn't get away with anything like that, so no, no overt attempt was made against me or anyone else I'm aware of.'

'So your answer to my question, Dr. Colbert, is that the defendant, even though he was visibly upset and made verbal threats, committed no violence whatever upon your person or any other person in your presence? By the way, just how many actual words did the defendant utter while you were with him? Roughly speaking, of course, Doctor. Can you give us some idea?'

'Not easily. Most of what he said

consisted of railing against his rotten luck.'

'Did you make an attempt to 'talk him down,' so to speak?'

'Certainly, I tried. But it was difficult to get through to him. But yes, I made every effort to calm him down.'

'By 'counter-threatening' him, Doctor?'

'I'm not sure I understand your meaning . . . '

'Did you tell him to expect some kind of consequences to his behavior?'

'At one point I suggested that if he didn't calm down on his own I might be forced to give him a sedative.'

'I think that in some arenas that could be considered a threat, Doctor.' Yeltoon began to rise in objection so she hurried on. 'But I take it that as a result of your intervention, the defendant eventually calmed down enough so that he could be booked and settled for the night?'

'He did.'

'Were you then able to give him a thorough medical examination? To test his heartbeat? His blood pressure? Did you take a urine specimen to determine the possibility of drug or alcohol impairment?'

'No, I was not asked by the authorities to undertake such testing at that time.'

'But did you run comprehensive tests on the defendant subsequently — or were any of the other medical personnel on duty that night asked to perform such tests?'

'No, not to my knowledge. Certainly no request was made of me to undertake such testing, and I am unaware of any other medical personnel called in to do so.'

'So when you gave us your opinion concerning Mr. Powell's so-called 'medical condition' at the time of his arrest, you're really just basing that opinion on a subjective 'impression' you had made without actually testing him. Thank you, Doctor, for your time and expertise.'

Yeltoon rose quickly to undertake damage control. 'I have just one or two more questions on redirect, Your Honor. Doctor, how did the defendant seem to you on the very first occasion when you saw him, shortly after the murder had been committed? How did he look to you?'

'Objection . . . '

'It goes to the defendant's attitude and appearance at that time, Your Honor . . . '

The judge paused. 'I think I'll allow it. We aren't on trial here today. We can be a little more flexible.'

Colbert moved smoothly on. 'The defendant seemed somewhat disheveled to me and there was blood on his clothing.'

'Thank you, Doctor. That will be all.'

Gail rose. 'Dr. Colbert, were you aware at the time that what you saw on the defendant's clothing were bloodstains?'

'Of course they could have been catsup or tomato juice stains, for all I knew. It was a just good guess later confirmed by the police.'

'But did you know or suspect that it *wasn't* his own blood?'

'Well, no. There's no way I could have known that at the time, and I don't believe it was ever confirmed to me later by the police.' He looked a little puzzled.

'Now, Doctor, please give us the benefit

of your experience and training. Upon reflection now, are you indeed so terribly shocked that Damon Powell should be 'upset' on that night, considering that he had been plucked off a country road, struck in the stomach without cause, and then placed under arrest for a murder he claims he knew nothing about and didn't commit?'

'Strike all that,' the judge said. 'That's not a question but a statement of opinion on Counsel's part.'

'I'd like an exception on that ruling, Your Honor. I feel it's most important. Dr. Colbert was one of the first persons to examine Mr. Powell after his arrest. And I, for one, would like a further delineation of his observations of the defendant's response to such treatment.'

'So noted for the record, but you will cease this line of questioning for now.' Gail inclined her head and returned to her seat.

Yeltoon rose. 'Just one or two more questions on redirect, if I may. Dr. Colbert, you've already told us that the defendant was cursing and shouting. Who was he cursing and what was he shouting?'

'Objection — hearsay.'

'Overruled. Continue.'

'Among many others, he seemed to be cursing at the girl who had been killed, Miss Seymour, I mean.'

'Please tell the Court the defendant's exact words, as nearly as you can remember them.'

Colbert looked uncomfortable. 'He said, on at least one occasion, 'That liar, Vivian.' Later on he said, 'Viv's just a little — ,' and he used a word in regard to her that I would rather not repeat in public.'

The courtroom was drenched in anticipatory silence.

The judge, having already played havoc with Gail's motion, turned now to Dr. Colbert and pounded the final nail in the coffin.

'So, the defendant called the dead girl by her name, did he?'

'At least twice — no, three times in my hearing, Your Honor. I keep notes of all my examinations, of course, and I refreshed my memory on this just before testifying.'

Gail got to her feet. 'May I request the Court's indulgence for a brief conference with my client?'

'By all means, Counselor.'

She bent her head toward Damon. 'Smile back at me while I talk to you, no matter what I say. We want everyone in this room to believe that you're giving me a reasonable explanation to everything that's been said — we've got to convince them all we're not worried about a thing.'

'That's a smart move,' Damon said. 'You sure are givin' 'em a bad tune!'

Gail reflected sourly that Damon's own particular yardstick for success depended solely on other people being made as uncomfortable as possible. He seemed to have no comprehension that Gail's motion for bail had gone south and that she'd gained little or no benefit by dragging everyone into court for her little 'fishing expedition.'

'Is there anything else I need to know about what went on between you and Dr. Colbert?'

'Nope. The fact is I really don't remember much about that part of it.'

'But you did use those words in connection with Vivian?'

'I honestly don't remember what I said.' He thought a moment. 'I'll tell you one thing though. No more cursing until this thing is over and I'm outta here!'

'Thank goodness,' Gail said. 'Now, smile when I turn away, as if I've just said something funny.'

She heard a chuckle from the table as she returned to the lectern. But she knew there wasn't much else to be retrieved from further questioning, so an unruffled Dr. Colbert was thanked and excused.

The judge spoke again.

'Does the Prosecution have any more witnesses?'

'I don't feel that they're necessary at this point, Your Honor.'

The judge made a beckoning motion to Gail. 'Will the Defense approach?'

And Gail knew immediately that the news would be bad.

'You've done well enough with this, Counselor,' the judge said. 'Your performance should convince the defendant's family that you're committed to fight for him . . . but I doubt if you should have expected much more out of today's session.'

Gail, her face coloring to deep red, asked quietly, 'Is Your Honor asking that I withdraw my motion?'

'Well, you're the moving party, and no one else can withdraw it for you.'

'And if I decline to withdraw?'

'Then I'll be forced to decide against you. You can withdraw without prejudice to any other motion, Counselor, and I shall so stipulate on the short form order that officially notes my finding.'

'Might I ask why the adverse decision?'

'You should know that questions like that don't get answered normally. But you're new to criminal law, so I'll make an exception. I know Dr. Colbert pretty well. And I'm pretty sure that if he sticks his neck out to make a point, there's very likely something in what he says.'

'I see.'

'I'm glad you do, Counselor. Now I'm going to adjourn court after you return to the defense table, and my disposition of this motion will appear tomorrow.'

Gail walked back to the table, ignoring Damon's questioning eyes. It did seem to her at this particular moment that judge, prosecutor, and witness were all part of a conspiracy with the sole purpose of steering the defendant directly into prison, or worse, to the execution chamber. She knew her discouragement wouldn't last though. She'd be ready to fight back at the next stage of the game.

5

Hugo Goldthwaite, Jr. was leaning against his flame-red sports car parked in front of the offices of Morin and Imlach when Gail joined him there the next afternoon.

'I don't know if this angle is the one you were talking about on the phone,' he began, 'but on account of what you said, I did some poking around and I think I've got through to somebody who'll tell you what you need to know. That doesn't mean he'd testify in court, of course.'

'Of course. But if there's a chance Vivian Seymour might have been involved in some hanky-panky, I want to check it out.'

She climbed into Hugo's car and he peeled out, causing Gail to put a cautionary hand on the dash. He drove swiftly to a somewhat seedy area not far from the downtown Seymour Mall. Half a dozen privately-owned motels dotted the landscape, their neon signs offering such delights as the obligatory swimming pool and 'TV in every room.'

Hugo swung in under the canopy at one of the less conspicuous of these, the Parkwood, and stood aside as Gail led the way into an establishment she'd never even heard of until now.

A rather large check-in desk took up the far corner of a narrow, gaudily-furnished lobby and Gail headed in that direction.

'Are you the owner?' she queried a skinny clerk sucking on a toothpick. He shook his head, shifted the pick to one side of his mouth, then yelled toward the open door behind the counter, 'Anse!'

A small man in his forties emerged. His tiny black eyes peered at her like a beetle's from the dark shadows. Gail reflected he surely was one of the ugliest individuals she had ever seen who made his living dealing with the public.

'I'm Anse Patillo,' he said by way of introduction, the sight of Hugo refreshing his memory. 'Come in. We can talk quiet back here. Al, I don't want to be disturbed now.'

Anse's office was so tiny that Hugo had

to lug in a third chair from the lobby.

'Please sit down, Miss,' Patillo said cheerfully then looked pointedly at Hugo. 'But where's this big-time lawyer I'm supposed to talk to?'

'Ms. Brevard here is the attorney who's handling the matter we discussed.'

'Oh, that's all right! Yes, I saw it in the paper, now you mention it. That's a great thing, you know, a girl being a lawyer and getting a big case like this.'

She supposed she should have thanked him profusely for being so liberal in his outlook toward women in the professions, but a polite incline of the head was all she could muster.

'When I was younger, the only girls in business were secretaries and receptionists — you know? Well, we live in different times and I don't mind it that much.' A crooked grin enhanced his features.

This time she did not entirely succeed in hiding her dismay.

'I don't blame you,' he said with a self-deprecating sigh, completely misinterpreting the reason for her grimace. 'With a face like mine, every night is

Halloween and I've got a mask on.' He laughed at his own joke. 'Some guys make it and some guys don't, I guess.'

The good part about the interview, Gail reflected, was that not only did this particular witness keep nothing to himself, but he insisted on offering even more gory details than she needed — or cared — to know.

Carefully, as if he were on the stand, she began to lead him up to the matter of greatest interest to her. 'Did some of these guys you're talking about come here with girls like Vivian Seymour?'

'Oh, didn't they, though!' The pearly gates of recollection had now been yanked wide open. 'When Hugo here came 'round to talk with me yesterday, he said that I've got the smallest place in the Mall area, so I probably get more of the crowd that doesn't want to be seen someplace like this. And he was right on the button, let me tell you!'

It made no sense at all to Gail, but it was apparent that this man had responded positively to all of Hugo's powers of persuasion.

'Really?' She batted her eyes in awe to urge him on. Hugo looked as if he might be sick.

'Oh, for sure!' Anse enthused. 'Vivian Seymour and her high-falutin' friends have been some of my most regular customers. There's probably a dozen of them in different rooms right now.' He snickered suggestively to Gail's horror. His bitterness about the handsome young men with all the pretty young girls was so persistent that Gail couldn't help turning away, embarrassed for the ugly little man.

'I don't think there ever was a guy who *couldn't* date the Seymour girl,' Patillo confided, warming to his topic. 'Once a month, at least, she was here with some guy or other. Even more often in the summer. Her father has lots of money, you know, and a lot of these guys didn't mind gettin' that close to the old man.'

Gail chose a point on the wall, far from the man's ugly features, and concentrated on it.

'F'r instance . . . One time I remember, I was walkin' down the hall and I caught a glimpse of her slinkin' along, her lipstick smeared and her dress a mess.' Gail concentrated on the spot even harder. ' . . . on her way down the hall from one room to another, playin' musical chairs, I guess.' He laughed.

'Did you ever see her on any of these occasions with the young man who's been accused of having killed her? You must have noticed his picture in the newspapers or on TV.'

'One of them looks just like another, if you ask me. But if you and Hugo want to take a look at the register, I won't stop you, Miss, er, Counselor. Just remember, these kids never sign in with their right names, so I don't suppose you'll find what you're looking for.'

'Thank you so much for saving us the time, Mr. Patillo,' she said. 'By the way, did anything out of the ordinary happen the last time you saw Vivian here, by any chance?'

'Nothin' real special. That was a couple of months ago, I guess.' He stopped. 'Yeah, I 'member now. Vivian got into a fight with one of her so-called friends in the coffee shop.'

'Do you have any idea what the argument was about?'

'She was goin' on about the fact that the other girl had worked for *her* father over the summer, so *she*, the other girl that is, didn't have any right to go after some guy Vivian wanted for herself. I remember I had to break up the two of them. It wasn't anything special, like I said. These kids often get into it like that. But that *was* the last time I saw her.'

'Do you recall the name of the guy they were fighting over . . . was he mentioned in your hearing?'

'Well, one guy's name is a lot like another, if you know what I mean (that seemed to be his favorite phrase). No way would I remember something like that.'

'What did the *other* girl look like?'

'I wouldn't remember that, either. Young girls look about the same to me nowadays, if you know . . . A sure sign I'm gettin' over the hill . . . .'

'Well, thank you very much, Mr. Patillo,' Gail broke in before he started rambling again. 'You've been a real help to us.'

'You understand, I hope, that while I'm willing to tell *you* all this stuff in confidence, I really can't go into court and spill my guts to the whole world. My stayin' in business depends on keepin' my mouth shut . . . *if you know what I mean.*'

Gail knew Patillo would have to testify, as a hostile witness, if necessary, if she decided to call him. And even if it briefly hurt his business, she was willing to bet the cretin would like nothing better than to be forced to go public with all the sordid details.

'I understand exactly how you feel, Anse.' He nodded appreciatively at her use of his given name. 'And I'm sure there won't be any need to inconvenience you any further. After all, you never really saw Vivian Seymour with Damon Powell, so that's the end of it, as far as I'm concerned.'

Gail knew that any testimony from Anse connecting Vivian with Damon would be far more useful to Turner than to Damon's defense, but she didn't say so.

'Well, all right then,' the innkeeper said. 'Glad if I could be of use, if you know what I mean.'

★ ★ ★

'You can see what a fun job I've got,' Hugo Goldthwaite said on the drive back to her office. 'I meet the *nicest* people.'

'I think you're underpaid,' she said. She thought a moment, then added, 'If Damon can't be linked to Vivian, then I'll make that point in court and get all the possible mileage I can out of it.'

'Okay. What's my next step?'

'See if you can find out who this other girl is — and if she might possibly be Damon's secret love interest.'

'I'll have to be careful about it — The Seymours and their friends have enough clout in this town to ruin anyone who brings them unwanted publicity,' Hugo said.

'Well, *I'm* not going to let myself be ruined, Hugo, and I think you have enough sense to stay out of harm's way as well.'

★ ★ ★

'I'm not sure what you can do with this information,' Hugo said when he checked in with Gail the next morning. 'But, one 'Laura Kincaid' is definitely 'V.'s little friend who worked for the 'S.'s last summer.'

'Hmmm . . . ' Gail thought about it a moment. 'Well, that in itself doesn't necessarily mean she was mixed up with our mutual 'friend.''

'But where there's smoke, there's bound to be fire, wouldn't you say?'

'That's your department.'

'And I guess it's also part of my job to clean up the mud I'll be stirring in the process.'

'I won't leave you out in the cold, Hugo. If anything happens, I'll just have you stashed into the tomb of the 'unknown detective.''

'Thanks a lot. Well, I'll let you know when — and if — I'm picked up and held incommunicado anywhere.'

'Trust me, Hugo. That's not going to happen — unless our opponents have completely lost their minds.'

'It's been my experience in this crazy ol' town that you never can be sure just what 'they' might do.'

'Get busy, Hugo. I'll be in touch.'

★ ★ ★

Gail made her way quickly past the knot of lawyers and their clients gathered on the first floor of the drafty old court-house. 'First calls' of the day had been completed, but those lawyers who weren't presently conducting trials were schmoozing with each other and stroking their anxious charges.

In little side rooms located on both sides of the corridor, paralegals were busily filing 'Notes of Issue' and 'Jury Demands,' and other motion papers. Here and there a clerk's voice called out 'Counselor,' as they retrieved files and forms. None of them seemed to understand why someone with a college education needed assistance in finding an index or calendar number within their jumbled files, or filling out the numerous complicated forms they required.

Gail poked her head inside the door of one of the clerk's offices. 'Pardon me, can you tell me which rooms are being used for an 'examination before trial' today?'

'Turn right at the end of this corridor, *Counselor*.'

Gail smiled sweetly. 'Thank you so much, *clerk*.'

The 'E.B.T.' room was claustrophobic, and held no more than six metal chairs pulled up tightly around a slightly battered bare wooden table. A man in his late forties was already perched on the edge of one chair. He was conservatively dressed, with button-down collar, striped silk tie, and the obligatory dark suit. Gail was acquainted with Charles Walton who, like herself, was just another corporation lawyer, and more accustomed to dealing with mundane matters far removed from a high-profile murder trial.

'I take it that you're representing the Seymours, Charles,' she said as she settled herself at the other end of the table, opening her briefcase and removing a sheaf of notes.

'Yes. Floyd — Mr. Seymour — is an old client of ours. He should be here shortly.'

And sure enough, just as he finished speaking, the door opened again and Floyd Seymour, a gray-haired man with a permanent scowl etched across his face, entered and took a seat. Following behind was a much younger man who immediately caught Gail's eye. There was no sign of Mrs. Seymour.

'My wife will not be attending today. I told her she had no need to encourage this blatant attempt to make her pain even worse than it is already.' Floyd Seymour's dark eyes challenged Gail. 'My attorney will produce the necessary medical excuses if you like. I am only here myself at his insistence, but I want to tell you, I'm not at all happy about . . . '

Gail intervened quickly. 'Mr. Seymour, I promise I'll try to keep this as brief and painless as possible, but the law requires our presence here, and I'm duty-bound to assist my client in his defense in any way I can.'

Seymour merely nodded his acceptance of the situation.

'I'm sure this won't take long, Uncle Floyd. I realize that we haven't met,' the younger man added, turning to Gail. 'I'm Nick Quintaine, Mr. Seymour's nephew.'

'What business do you have here?'

'I'm only here to lend my uncle moral support. Other than that, I'll try to stay out of it.'

Gail nodded. 'Then I hope you won't interfere with my questions.' Nick Quintaine seemed inclined to act as a peacemaker in the present situation, and he might be useful in that regard.

'I'm sure we can keep things from getting out of hand.' His deep voice was as charming as his looks, and Gail had to force her attention away from him as the court stenographer entered.

'We'll start now, Mr. Seymour. Your full name is Floyd Armbruster Seymour?'

Seymour glanced skeptically at Charles Walton. 'Was I brought down here to be asked trivial questions and then have them answered for me?'

'Only at the beginning of the interview, Floyd,' Walton said hastily. 'As soon as the questions begin to deal with details of the case itself, you'll be asked to respond.'

'You're married to Nancy Walton Stafford?' Gail continued. 'I am.' She suddenly realized that the middle name explained Seymour's choice of an attorney for this proceeding. Charles Walton was almost certainly a relative of some sort, and a member of the network of the Seymours' influential social and business friends who seemed to be arrayed against her client.

Seymour muttered under his breath. 'I'm furious about this . . . '

Gail ignored his comment and continued smoothly: 'How long have you and your wife been married? Twenty-three years. You are self-employed as a builder? Yes, I am. Have there been any children by this marriage? One child, a daughter. Do you refer to nineteen-year-old Vivian Walton Seymour? Yes. Is she recently deceased by foul play? Yes. Did your daughter live at home? Yes.'

'Another minute of this idiocy,' Seymour snapped, 'and I'm out of here.'

'Then I'll call the Cathcart *Sun* and grant them an interview,' Gail said just as quickly in return, 'claiming that I am unable to get a fair hearing of this matter in this town because you refuse to play by the rules.'

Nick put out a calming hand and wordlessly held Seymour's arm a moment, an action for which Gail thanked him with her eyes.

'In a minute, Mr. Seymour,' she went on, 'I'm going to ask you the sort of questions that no father should ever have to answer, let alone a recently bereaved one. I consider it vital, though, to make sure that justice, in every sense of the word, is done in this case — justice to all involved.'

'Go to blazes!'

Once again she ignored the outburst. 'Was there ever any friction between you and your daughter?' This time she paused to allow him to respond.

'No, none at all!'

'One word responses aren't required here, Mr. Seymour, as they are in a regular court of law. You're entirely free to expand on the subject as you see fit.'

'My answer is the one I just gave you.'

He glared pointedly at Walton while he spoke, as if he was waiting for his own lawyer to make objections on his behalf.

'Are you saying, then, Mr. Seymour, that there was *never* any friction at all between the two of you? No arguments? No bones of contention?'

'None! Never! My Vivian was a good girl!'

'And was there ever any mild disagreement between you about the boys she was seeing?'

'None.'

'Do you know if Mrs. Seymour ever complained to your daughter about her activities?'

'Mrs. Seymour didn't need to.'

'Before the recent tragic events, did you ever hear the name of Damon Powell?'

'No, I did not!' He stood. 'I came here as ordered by some idiot judge who won't be re-elected to office, believe me. I will not have my daughter's good name dragged through the dirt by any of your ridiculous insinuations that she had any kind of relationship with that criminal. No cruel assumptions are going to be made about her. And believe me, whoever does make those accusations in public will have to answer to me and to the good people of Cathcart!'

'Am I to take that as a threat, Mr. Seymour?'

But Seymour turned on his heel and abruptly left the room. On Gail's cue, the stenographer put away her things and quietly exited as well.

Nick Quintaine shrugged and smiled ruefully at Gail as he got to his feet to follow his uncle. And in spite of the somewhat unsatisfactory conclusion to this particular procedure, Gail didn't think the day had been a complete loss.

Walton was gathering up the contents of his briefcase, too. 'Sorry about all that, Gail. I tried to prepare him for this, but the whole mess has been just a little much for all of us.'

'That's all right, Charles. I know you tried.'

In spite of her best efforts, Gail knew that she had alienated Seymour, who, in retaliation, would probably make some attempt to destroy her legal career here in

Cathcart, no matter how the trial turned out. It would be a shame if that happened, but she had never entered into any enterprise halfheartedly in her entire life — and she wasn't about to begin now.

★ ★ ★

As Gail reached the lobby, she recognized a reporter from the *Sun* talking animatedly to an older man. As soon as she appeared, the newspaperman pointed to her and then walked quickly away.

The man moved toward her. He was in his sixties, with a high forehead, a thick head of curly graying hair and bright blue probing eyes. He looked vaguely familiar, as if she had seen him in or about the court house.

'You're the lawyer who's trying the Powell case.' It wasn't a question.

Gail replied politely. 'If you have any information to offer about the case, why not make an appointment with me at my office?'

He laughed. 'But we're here together, now!'

'Then why not give me the short version, *now?*' Gail glanced pointedly at her watch.

'Let's just say,' he eyed the various legal pros bustling through the hallway, 'that I'm one of Cathcart's most avid trial buffs.'

Gail nodded. He was one of those curiosities, usually retired, who made a hobby of attending trials for the fun of it, especially those with sensational features, like the Powell case.

Gail was about to excuse herself as courteously as she could, when one of her colleagues stopped and smiled at the newcomer.

'How're you doin' today, Judge?' the passerby asked, offering his hand.

'Jes' settin' up and takin' nourishment, m'boy. Thanks for asking.'

Gail was getting tired of sparring with this guy. As soon as the other attorney moved on, she said, a bit testily, 'If you're a legal pro and you have any positive information or advice for me, I'll be only too happy to make time for you.'

'Good, good. Now we're gettin' some-where.' He rubbed his hands together in anticipation. 'What say we mosey over to the *Third Call*? Are you game? Fine.'

The place to which he referred had been named thusly because there were traditionally no more than 'two calls' to a court calendar. The 'third call' was then outside the calendar, *i.e.*, outside the jurisdiction of the courtroom. Lawyers and legal pros gathered in the upscale restaurant daily for lunch, and to hold impromptu meetings with colleagues and others in the adjacent dim and discreet bar.

Gail's cheeks were pinched with the wintry cold by the time she and her companion had walked the two blocks to the popular watering hole. Her presence there drew no more than a brief nod from the headwaiter, but then a broad smile was trotted out for her companion.

'Ms. Brevard and I are only going to have coffee and conversation,' the judge said with a significant pause before the last two words. 'Is my usual table free? Thanks.'

They were led without further ado to a comfortable corner table separated from the others. Gail began to believe that it might be instructive to hear what this man had to say.

'Except for eight years on the bench, I've been a criminal lawyer my whole working career,' he began by way of explanation. He now introduced himself as Zachary Ulrich. 'Call me Zack. I'm retired from the bench now because of a weakened heart, but that doesn't mean I've lost interest in the law. Nowadays, I've got nothing much better to do than hang out around the courthouse and commiserate with the defense teams.'

Gail was beginning to have a glimmer of understanding as to why he had waylaid her. 'And you think you can help me?'

'That's as good a way of putting it as any other,' Zack nodded. 'This particular case has been foisted off on you, even though you are totally inexperienced in criminal matters. You have to ask yourself if that isn't an attempt by the powers that be in this town to 'railroad' the defendant while not ruffling any establishment feathers while they're at it.'

'Yes, that's the way I see it, too. Whatever it is 'they' think they're doing, I'm not sure. But if it makes any difference to you, I may just have ruffled a few of those 'local feathers.''

'Good for you.' Ulrich looked thoughtful for a moment. 'But what's to be done about it now? What else *can* be done, I should say.'

'I get the distinct feeling that you're on the verge of making a suggestion.'

'What *I* think you need,' he went on, 'is help in preparing for each day's session and in reviewing the proceedings afterwards, not to mention an everyday conference here, for instance, at lunchtime. How do *you* feel about that suggestion?'

Gail grinned and threw out her hand. 'Motion granted!'

6

'Are both sides ready for *voir dire*?' Judge West demanded impatiently. A senior jurist, he appeared to be none too pleased about being assigned to this case.

'The Prosecution's ready, Your Honor.' Turner stood to take charge of his case.

'The Defense is ready as well, Your Honor,' Gail responded from her side of the aisle.

West nodded at the attorneys then turned towards the members of the jury pool who had been herded up into the courtroom from the nether recesses of the building. They sat, huddled together, looking like so many deer caught in the headlights of the judge's piercing glare.

After introducing both the Special Prosecutor and the Counsel for the Defense, he began: 'You each will be examined in detail by me and by each of the attorneys, in what will sometimes seem to you to be a repetitive process, and our mutual decisions in regard to your eligibility to sit on this trial will be made jointly and in consideration of your responses.' He spoke with authority and at some length about the nature of the action before them and their duties and responsibilities as jurors. He finally paused, looked over his notes once more, then announced: 'We will now begin the questioning procedure.' The clerk, with a flourish of ceremony, reached into a box filled with cards bearing the names of each candidate and lifted the first one out. That name was called, and a heavy-set man stood and moved, somewhat self-consciously, to the witness chair where he took a seat and waited apprehensively.

'Your vocation, Mr. Martindale?' the judge asked. 'How do you make your living?'

'I'm a plumber.'

'This is likely to become a celebrated trial, with the publicity that has already been involved. It might become necessary to keep the jury in a hotel for the length of the proceedings. Could you accept that?'

'If I must.'

'Do you suffer from any major illnesses that would prevent you sitting on such a trial? Heart trouble? Any other maladies of the sort?'

'I've got a bit of arthritis, Judge,' he responded doubtfully, 'but that's all.'

The judge nodded and glanced at Turner. 'Continue your *voir dire*, Mr. Redland.'

Turner took a stance in front of the witness box, smiling with self-confidence, his handsome head cocked rakishly to one side. His voice and manner were quiet and respectful, immediately putting the questioned man at ease. As he would do in every instance, Turner began by asking Martindale if he was for or against the death penalty.

'Do you feel that you could try this case on the issues as set forth by the court, Mr. Martindale?' he queried. 'And do you agree or disagree that the defendant is entitled to every possible advantage, for example, because of his youth?'

'I wouldn't pay no 'tention to the age

of somebody who might've — uh, killed somebody.'

'Would you be able to vote for the death penalty in this trial?'

'If I thought it was the right thing to do.'

Redland considered the response for a moment then turned towards West. 'To save time, Your Honor, the Prosecution will accept this juror without further questioning.'

Gail stood and shuffled the papers on her table. She was mulling over the advice she had received from Zack Ulrich — but Mr. Martindale didn't seem to fall into any of Zack's 'forbidden' categories.

'Would you be upset, Mr. Martindale,' she ventured, 'if the trial brought out some unsavory details about certain people in our community who are thought of as fine and upstanding citizens?'

'I guess it would depend on the details.'

'Would it be upsetting to you, for instance,' she pursued, 'if certain portions of this trial dealt with the sexual habits of such people?'

He considered a moment. 'I don't think so, Miss.'

'Would you have any strong objections to hearing details of perversion, if those matters should arise during the course of the trial?'

There was a little murmur amongst the captive audience, and Gail was tempted to steal a glance at Turner to see if he was swallowing these red herrings she was so generously casting at his feet.

'I wouldn't object, I suppose, if it was necessary for the trial, I mean.' Martindale pulled a none-too-white handkerchief from his front shirt pocket and nervously mopped at his shiny brow.

Gail asked a few more pointed questions then came to a quick decision.

'Defense challenges for cause. Article two-two, subsection five, of the State Code of Criminal Practice: 'if a prospective juror's beliefs clash with . . . ''

Judge West held up a hand. 'I'm familiar with the Code, Counselor, and I think that you may be stretching the word 'beliefs' about as far as it will go. In the circumstances, however — I'll allow it.'

Gail nodded. She had done well, she thought, but other prospective jurors would also have to be weighed and measured, and fatal errors still could be made. She had no idea if she'd be satisfied when the jury selection process was over and done with, but she hoped Turner was a little less sure of himself for once.

'Thank you, Your Honor.' She smiled to show she was grateful for his ruling.

'Proceed,' the judge responded, turning to his clerk, and Gail couldn't help noticing that the judge definitely had not smiled back at her.

The clerk called out another name, and Turner Redland rubbed his hands in anticipation of the joust to come.

* * *

'You gave your occupation as 'retired,' Mr. Kowalski,' Gail said to the second prospective juror when her turn came. 'How did you earn a living before you retired?'

'I was a messenger, then a salesman . . . and I worked in a shoe factory . . . '

'But just *before* you retired, Mr.

Kowalski, what was your occupation at *that* time?'

The man shrugged. 'I was a police officer.'

'Do you think that you could forget all your experience of police work in order to serve on this jury?'

'I'd be glad to try.'

'Nevertheless, I'm worried that some development in the course of the trial might make you compare events with your past work as a patrolman and, perhaps, arouse some prejudice or other. We'll thank and excuse you, sir.'

Turner turned to Gail. 'Is this a peremptory challenge?'

She hesitated. She was entitled to only fifteen peremptory challenges, too few in her opinion, but she had been made aware of the Court's desire to appear as if time was being saved. Here was a chance to show that she, too, was interested in the shortest possible disposition of the action before them.

'It is a peremptory challenge, yes.'

She wished she hadn't seen Turner's satisfied smirk at having bullied her into using a peremptory when the same result could have been obtained a little more deftly. She chalked it up to experience. Next time she'd know better.

★   ★   ★

'Miss Bazlioni,' Gail began. 'I couldn't help but wonder at the way you looked at my learned colleague when you first saw him here.'

'Oh, there was nothin' to *that*,' the woman responded, a bit nervously.

'But have you ever met him before, perhaps socially? If the answer is that you have, Miss Bazlioni, it is best to tell us now so that it won't be necessary to shuffle the jury later on.'

'We — yes, I have met Mr. Redland.'

There was a soft but pointed slurring of 'met.'

'Socially?'

'You might call it that.'

'Please excuse me, but we must have the facts for our records: how well do you know the Special Prosecutor?'

Her answer was too low to be heard,

even in the suddenly stone-quiet court-room, but every onlooker was aware of Turner's sudden gasp and saw the truth in the woman's beet-red face.

'The defense accepts Miss Bazlioni, but deplores the shortness of the Special Prosecutor's memory.' Gail turned back to her table with a broad grin.

Redland mumbled gruffly. 'Challenge for cause.'

Judge West asked dryly, 'Well now, have you got any law on that, Mr. Special Prosecutor?'

* * *

Turner had just taken his seat after questioning the next juror when a messenger entered the courtroom and approached him with a note. He glanced at it, scrawled a few words on it, and gestured to a clerk to pass it on to Gail who was by then standing at the lectern.

Redland had scribbled, 'I probably owe you a favor for old time's sake' across a corner of a typed memo indicating that Harvey Krempel, the prospective juror

109

then seated in the dock, was a known offender, although with no convictions.

Wondering if the message was a put-up job on Turner's part or if the sex offense business was genuine, Gail also realized she would use up another of her precious peremptory challenges if she acted on the information.

'The defense accepts this juror without question.' In for a penny . . .

But Turner didn't challenge the juror either, telling her she'd probably made a different mistake this time. She was right, as Zack explained to her over a long lunch at the *Third Call*. 'I know who this Krempel *really* is. He was a staunch witness for the Prosecution when I defended some nut case a while back.'

'In other words, this fellow will more than likely sympathize with the Prosecution, and now I can't get him off the jury?'

'You *can* have him kicked off, but then you'll look indecisive and as if you're wasting the Court's time again, which is something like the eleventh deadly sin. Don't forget, this joker has been accepted by both sides now. On the other hand, he's only one voice out of twelve.'

'It's a shame you're not at the defense table with me.'

'You'll get more sympathy if you're the only lawyer up there,' Zack pointed out to her. 'A plucky young maiden, single-handedly fighting against the full force of the highly-experienced Special Prosecutor. You can take my word for it.'

★   ★   ★

'Do you think that you could try a case with unpleasant details?' Gail was asking prospective juror number twenty-six. 'If such details are necessary, of course.'

'I think so,' Mr. Ruiz said, a little uncertainly.

'The jury will certainly be shown some pictures of a corpse, Mr. Ruiz,' Gail went on, trying to pinpoint her gut reason for not being entirely satisfied with his responses. 'Could you tolerate that?'

'I suppose.'

'You'll have to hear testimony about extreme damage the victim suffered . . .'

'If I have to listen, I'll listen.'

'Then you don't object to detailed medical testimony, Mr. Ruiz?'

The man hesitated. 'You mean — like about post-mortem stuff, that kind of thing?'

'Yes, that kind of thing.' Once more Gail's finer instincts proved out.

'I'm not sure I can, lady. You see, my missus died suddenly a couple of months ago, and the doctor said he had to cut her up like that after. I got so *mad* that I swore I never woul . . . ' He paused, tears filling his eyes.

'Thank you very much, Mr. Ruiz. That's all the questions I have for you at this time.'

She waited as Judge West added in an uncharacteristically kind manner, 'I think we'll excuse you from hearing this case, sir. Thank you for your service. Please return to the jury room and wait to be called for some other matter.'

7

Zack and Gail were comfortably seated in the living area of the suite Gail had taken in the Cathcart Hotel for the duration of the trial. The hotel was close to the courthouse, allowing her to dash over during the various recesses and breaks to take a shower and change. Often, she just wanted a chance to put her feet up with a cup of coffee or tea and relax as she reviewed the day's proceedings and plan her next move. It was certainly more convenient than driving all the way across town to the suburbs, and it also allowed her to keep the relevant files and paperwork close at hand without carrying everything back and forth daily.

'See if you can get that black guy seated next,' Zack urged, after going over the list of prospects again.

'Why him?'

'In my experience, most minorities are suspicious of authority. Turner knows that and he won't be happy about this one.'

So, at the beginning of the afternoon session Gail rose to address John Waters, the lone black candidate for Powell's jury. 'The defense accepts Mr. Waters without further questioning, Your Honor. Welcome aboard, Mr. Waters.'

Waters eyed her warily without comment. But it wasn't until the next day's lunch break that Gail discovered the truth of the matter. Waters was the chair of the Cathcart Law and Order League, a group of like-minded conservatives who believed that most criminals were being coddled by 'do-gooder' liberals. Gail was appalled at what she had done and said as much to Zack as they began their meal.

'He's goin' to want to hang our kid up by the thumbs,' Ulrich speculated aloud as soon as Gail had passed the information along. 'Redland put on such a good performance of hesitating about the guy that we fell right into his trap.'

'I guess *we* shouldn't have trusted to stereotypes so much,' Gail said, eyes cast down resignedly at her plate. She was more than a little angry, both at herself, but also at Zack — and she made a mental note to carefully vet any future advice from him — or anyone else for that matter — for the duration of the trial.

*   *   *

The next morning, just as court was being convened, Damon's mother once more cornered Gail for a short 'chat.' This time Mrs. Powell was adorned in a blue taffeta cocktail dress, which looked cheap — and highly inappropriate for her role as mother of the defendant. Mr. Powell, in plainer attire, hovered in her wake.

'I *really* don't want to second-guess you, dear,' she said, 'but as I told you, Mr. Powell and I have some lawyer friends — and one of them said that your first move in the case ought to have been to ask for a 'change of venue,' as he called it.'

Gail took a deep breath and counted to ten. Even if that suggestion might have been appropriate at the outset which, in her opinion, wasn't the case, it was completely out of line to pursue it now, especially since ten jurors had been seated with only two more, plus the alternates, remaining to be chosen.

'Thank you so much for passing your friend's suggestion on to me,' Gail said, managing a smile.

'Would you like to consult with him? He promised me he'd make himself available if you want his help.'

'I'll certainly keep that in mind,' Gail said. A tear made its way down Mrs. Powell's powdered cheek. She was obviously trying to do *anything* to aid in her son's defense. Gail started to reach out a sympathetic hand toward the older woman — but she had never been comfortable with that sort of gesture, and quickly changed it to a handshake. All of her compassion seemed to have been taken up lately in dealing with Erle — there was nothing left to spare. Mrs. Powell looked away in embarrassment. Had the difficult woman actually understood some part of Gail's gesture?

One result of the meeting was that Gail found herself in no mood to take any more sass from Damon. As she sat down at their table she noticed he was wearing some kind of crude pendant around his neck. 'What *is* that?' she snapped.

'It's a good luck charm. I've been hiding it under my shirt up to now.'

'Well stick it back under your shirt again,' she ordered, 'or I'll yank it off and toss it in the trash,'

Damon took one look at her angry face and did as he had been told.

*　*　*

'So, at last we have the complete jury before us,' said Zack, pulling a yellow pad of paper from his brief case and uncapping his favorite fountain pen. 'From these twelve, three are women. Four are Catholics, one is Jewish, and seven are Protestant.' He made quick notes as he spoke. 'One is Black, one is French, and three have Central European origins. We must presume that the ancestors of the rest were in this country when the natives were still throwin' stones at George Washington.'

The two were holed up in Gail's hotel room. At her request the management had brought in an oblong conference table and chairs and a combination Fax/copy machine, as well as a standard DSL hookup for her laptop. She also had arranged with young Hugo to run daily checks for listening devices, just to be on the safe side. Other necessities were messengered back and forth from the firm's nearby offices as needed.

'Six are Republicans, three are Democrats, and the other three haven't got any party affiliations that they've declared. Two are stay-at-home housewives, five are blue-collar workers, and the rest can be considered white-collar. Two might be prejudiced *against* Redland and seven more are likely to be open-minded about the whole matter. It's quite an achievement, Gail, to get seven open-minded people on a jury in a headline murder trial, especially these days.'

'I hope you're right,' Gail said. 'But what do any of those statistics really mean? And how can we use them to our advantage?'

Zack thoughtfully scratched his head then grinned at her quizzically. 'I wish I knew, Gail. I sure wish I knew!'

8

Phil Osborn had to restrain himself to keep from jumping up and stalking out of the restaurant. He frowned across the table at his companion and tried to stop looking annoyed.

His dining partner was Frances Hector, a dark-eyed, well-worn blonde in her thirties. Fran was blessed with a decent shape, but she didn't have much of a knack for dressing it. Osborn, who sold men's clothing for a living, prided himself on being aware of the latest in fashion, women's as well as men's. Fran's ineptitude was irritating to Phil, but he didn't want to risk losing the possibility for some kind of interlude between them — so he kept his mouth shut and stayed put.

Fran hadn't been listening to his efforts at conversation. She was gazing about her — at the room, the well-dressed diners, the serve staff in their starched uniforms.

Her lips were parted in an ecstasy of awe.

'*This* is where all the lawyers come for lunch,' she whispered. 'I suppose it's too late in the evening to see anyone who's anyone though.'

'Sure, it's too late.' Osborn had been one of the last jurors seated on the Damon Powell trial. He hadn't been overly eager for this assignment, but the idea had been growing on him steadily over the last day or so. He'd take some time off work, and those chintzy bosses at *Magnus's for Men* would have to pay him for every second of it. Plus which, he'd pocket the measly juror's fee. 'I guess we'll be seeing plenty of lawyers for the next few weeks.' He might as well pay ol' Frannie a little more attention and make himself seem easy to get along with.

'Yes,' she sighed. 'But *you'll* be a real juror and I'm nothing more than the first alternate. Ya' know, I *always* wanted to go into the law myself, but my folks didn't have enough money to send me to school — and I never could force myself to do the 'work all day, then go to law school at night' thing. Do you s'pose that makes me lazy?'

Yes, he thought savagely, *yes, you're lazy, all right.* 'Of course not, Fran. A lot of people just haven't got the energy it takes to put in eight hours a day on some stupid job and another three or four at night hittin' the books or listenin' to some idiot professor mouthin' off. It's a hundred percent understandable.'

'And there always were so many things to do *after* work when I was younger,' she added thoughtfully. 'So that's *one* reason it isn't me who is taking charge of the defense in an important case like this one.'

She had stayed as close to the legal profession as she could, though, and at present she was working in a local law firm as a receptionist. During her employment there she had engaged in endless curiosity about the lawyers' various cases while doing as little as possible of her own work. The salary wasn't bad and, all things considered, she thought of herself as pretty lucky. 'I always hoped that one of these days I'd be a juror on a big case like this one,' she added dreamily over the last of her chicken *tetrazzini*. 'A *real* juror, not just an alternate.'

'It's a shame that this case isn't more interesting.' Osborn felt he had to make some response. 'A kid goes to see a girl and there's trouble between them. Next thing you know he turns on her and the girl turns up dead. There can't be any real argument about who did it.'

Her eyes flicked his way a bit angrily. 'We're not supposed to talk between ourselves about the case until a verdict has been reached,' she said.

'You want to stick with all the rules, Fran, it's okay by me.'

She attacked her food again, but didn't stay silent for long. 'All the same, Phil, you shouldn't have already made up your mind if the defendant is guilty or innocent.'

'There's no doubt about who did it — in my opinion.' He bit through the buttered roll in his pudgy hand. He was getting tired of this discussion, and tired of her. He wished she'd just shut her yap so they could finish this dreary meal.

Fran didn't say anything, but her face was flushed right to the tips of her ears.

She was more than a little outraged that anyone in his right mind could reach a conclusion in direct opposition to the orders that had been issued to them by the judge.

Osborn pushed himself to be a better host. 'I'd be willin' to change my mind — if that good-lookin' lawyer dame can persuade me otherwise,' he added smugly.

But Fran wasn't much soothed by that thought either, and Phil, unfortunately, failed to notice the quick look of disgust that passed across her features, a look that was far from friendly.

'We don't have to be in court until ten tomorrow morning,' he observed casually. 'What say we take in a movie? There's a new comedy showing . . . '

Fran agreed readily and the two were soon sharing popcorn and laughing companionably. He had decided the simplest approach was best, and wasted no time. 'Let's go back to my hotel,' he said as they left the theater. 'We can have a drink and relax a bit.'

'I didn't know you lived in a hotel,' she said.

He explained that he had taken a room at the Copeland for the duration of the trial.

'I've only been inside the Copeland once, but I remember it as a very nice facility,' Fran said. 'You drive on ahead and I'll follow.'

'I need to go up and grab my credit card,' he said as they walked out of the hotel parking area together a while later. 'See ya' in the bar in about ten minutes or so?'

'Fine. That'll give me just enough time to visit the ladies' room and freshen my makeup.'

Phil had booked a big room with a king-sized bed and a comfy lounge area. He looked about with approval, relishing the idea of sharing all that with the curvaceous Fran.

He waited a few more minutes then phoned her at the bar. 'Ya' know. It just occurred to me. Why don't you just come up here instead? We'd be a lot more comfortable . . . '

'To your room, you mean?'

'Yes. We can order from room service

and avoid the crowd.'

'Well . . . I suppose so . . . '

'Fine. I'm in Room 215.'

Frances Hector responded with a purr. 'Actually, I'm really glad you suggested this, Phil. This is just what I was hoping you had in mind.'

He whistled happily after breaking the connection. For just a moment there he had doubted she would be willing to come to his room. But his initial take on the situation had been dead-on, and a pleasant few weeks of fun and games during the progress of the trial stretched in front of him.

A sudden knock on the door broke his reverie. Phil was stunned that she had made it up the elevator in so short a time. Well, he did like his women to be punctual.

The woman on the other side of the door, however, was definitely *not* Frances Hector. Phil found himself gazing open-jawed at a comely young thing in her mid- to late-teens, sporting a luscious figure — and little else. And he was positive Fran would never be caught dead in sky-high stilettos like those.

'You've got the wrong room, Miss,' he said, somewhat regretfully.

But the girl just stood her ground and smiled. 'I'm sure I've got the right room.'

Then she stretched up on tip-toe and kissed him full on the mouth.

'Look. I'm tellin' ya you're in the wrong room,' he reiterated, flinging the door open a little wider and motioning her out. 'I didn't ask you here.'

'But now that I am here, surely you can make the most of it,' she teased.

'I don't fool around with women I don't know.'

'Oh but you know you'll like *me*,' she murmured, and threw her arms around his neck once more, dragging his face down to hers.

Suddenly she raised both hands in the air and screamed like a banshee, turning her head toward the hallway so that the noise would carry further.

Phil now realized she was setting him up. This was obviously a blackmail attempt, but he had no intention of paying her off. He had worked way too hard for his twice-a-month paycheck to throw it away like

126

this. He made a move for the house phone, ready to call downstairs and have her tossed out, but because he'd had his eyes on her all the time, he failed to notice a sudden movement in the hall.

And there was Fran, standing in the doorway. She glanced in, darting her eyes, back and forth, from Phil to the girl. 'What's going on here, Phil?'

He halfway expected Fran to turn away in outrage and head back for the elevator, but she just stood there with feet planted, brows raised, and eyes a little wide, as she waited for her question to be answered.

'He tricked me up here,' the interloper said between hiccupping sobs. 'He tried to take my clothes off.' And she gestured down to her dress, which she herself had ripped in the scuffle.

Phil could not believe that a mature woman like Fran would take this girl to be anything but what she was. He looked on in amazement as a glance of sympathy darted from Fran's dark eyes toward the young woman.

He began speaking, in a brisk, business-like manner. 'Now listen. I'm callin' the house dick to throw you outta here.'

The girl's sobs went up a notch. There was some more stirring in the hall. Frances was asking the girl, 'Did he force . . . ?' But she didn't bother to finish her thought. Her eyes narrowed as she observed the traces of lipstick on his mouth. He could taste it — a little like bubble-gum . . .

Just then a beefy looking man in his fifties appeared in the hallway, shouldering Frances aside, but speaking to her out of the corner of his mouth at the same time.

'What's the problem here?'

Ordinarily, Phil would have welcomed another man on his side, but he was beginning to feel crowded and annoyed. 'What makes this any business of yours?' he asked.

The stranger responded by striding into the room and thrusting his ID in Phil's face. 'This does,' he growled.

'Let me see it closer up,' Phil said, trying to maintain his control. He barked into the receiver in his hand. 'Front desk? Is there a detective in your employ by the name of Fred Vandermeer? Heavy-set, probably in his fifties . . . There is? Thank you. No, that's all.'

Phil returned Fred's ID, vaguely relieved that someone with experience in this sort of thing was here to help him out of his dilemma. He chose his next words carefully. 'This . . . *girl*, the younger one . . . is trying to scam me.'

But Vandermeer was having none of it. 'Did she ask you for money? No? Well then, I don't see how you can claim she was scamming you. Because of the uncertain nature of this disturbance, I'm afraid I'm going to have to ask you to check out immediately, sir. We don't normally care if you entertain a circus of acrobats, but if you can't do it without upsetting the other guests, we have to ask you to leave.'

'Can't *you* tell she's a scam artist?'

'Look bud, it don't matter one way or t'other to me. You're still gonna have to check out.'

'I'll have a talk with the manager before I do,' Phil muttered.

'Suit yourself. I'll give you fifteen

minutes to pack up — then you're gone.' With that, the detective turned and escorted the girl out with him. Interestingly, Fran followed along after them.

Phil was only vaguely aware of Fran tossing him one last defiant glare out of eyes that glinted wickedly. And her lips were stretched taut in the faint beginnings of a smile.

The next morning he began to comprehend fully what had actually taken place.

At a little after ten, just after he had taken his assigned seat in the jury box, a clerk appeared at his side and motioned him into an adjoining anteroom. Surprised and somewhat perplexed, Phil waited there for further instructions.

Then the judge — what was his name, West? — entered and looked at Phil with thinly disguised disdain. Osborn found himself on the point of asking if his tie was on crooked, but changed his mind when he realized who else had entered the room.

Plunking his massive butt down in a leather-bound visitor's chair, his shiny face reflecting the still morning sky through the dusty window, was none other than Fred Vandermeer, the house dick who had caused Phil so much grief at the Copeland Hotel the evening before.

'That's the man,'Vandermeer said firmly, gesturing in Phil's direction. 'Checked in under the name of Osborn.'

'Repeat to him, please, exactly what you just told me,' Judge West said.

Vandermeer then noted that Mr. Osborn here, had brought an unregistered guest up to his room at the Copeland Hotel, where he, Mr. Vandermeer, was employed as a private detective. Mr. Osborn then attacked the girl, who appeared to be under-age. Sadistically-inclined men, he added, always seem to think that such women are fair game because they can't fight back.

'Any comments, Mr. Osborn?' the judge asked evenly.

Phil stuck to the truth as best he could, although some of the details still seemed a bit hazy to him. He deliberately left Frances's name out of it. He was still hoping, in a muzzy sort of way, that his omission would be appreciated by her later on. Perhaps he could still salvage something out of the relationship.

Judge West nodded. 'I'm half inclined to believe you, Osborn. The Copeland is an expensive place, but the staff isn't nearly as careful as it might be about who is allowed to loiter about inside.'

Vandermeer opened his mouth to object, but on second thought, changed his mind and merely shrugged. The best thing, he thought, was to let the judge have his say rather than argue the point.

'But under these particular circumstances,' West continued, 'I've got no choice about the action I must take. If either the Prosecution or the Defense gets wind of this, they could wait until near the end then bring it up in an effort to overthrow the outcome of the trial. I doubt they'd get very far, but they could cause considerable upset and delays with such a ploy — which no one wants. Justice delayed, as the saying goes, is justice denied. A new trial might have to be arranged. And even if it should be determined that the girl's claims were untrue, there still could be all kinds of havoc raised over this.'

'So you're kickin' me off the jury?' Phil stared at West in disbelief.

'I don't have any choice in the matter, Mr. Osborn. I'm going to arrange instead for the first alternate juror to take your place.'

As Osborn trudged slowly out of the building he halted in mid-stride. Suddenly it all came clear to him. The first alternate juror was none other than *Miss Frances Hector*! She may not be a lawyer, but Frances was now a juror — in a really big case. A *real* juror, not just an alternate!

Phil just stood there on the steps lost in thought, as lawyers and their clients made their way around him, like an island in a stream. Had Fran set him up? Had she actually planned all this out from the very beginning? Had *she* hired the girl to go to his room? And then had she notified Vandermeer about the so-called 'disturbance?' And later, when she left with Vandermeer, did she persuade him to go to the judge and spill his guts?

Sure, Phil reflected. Sure. She had done all that. And he had been such a fool about it!

It was really weird, the whole bit! And so was Frances Hector weird, crazier than anyone he'd ever known. He knew one thing. If he ever saw her again, he'd turn tail and run in the opposite direction!

And if he was ever called for jury duty again, he'd get himself excused. He had figured out that the lawyers weren't likely to accept anyone who sincerely didn't want to serve, so there wouldn't be any problem with that. He knew one thing only. He'd had more than enough of this so-called justice system.

By six o'clock in the evening, he had spent five hours back on the selling floor at *Magnus's for Men*. He had sold four high-priced sports jackets and two suits. And as often as he told himself he didn't like the job, he was feeling pretty good about himself by the time he left the store that evening, retrieved his car from the lot, and drove back home to lick his wounds.

* * *

Following a brief discussion with both sets of attorneys in chambers, Judge West ordered Frances Hector to move from the first alternate's chair to Osborn's seat in the jury box. And, for a while, the importance of this change didn't seem particularly relevant.

* * *

Judge John West made himself comfortable, looked out over his captive audience, then asked each of the attorneys, 'Is there any further business before we call in the jury?'

Redland stood. 'One small matter for the People, if the Court pleases.'

There was a ripple of whispered comments from the spectator seats.

'The viewers will refrain from speaking amongst themselves,' West said. 'You are here as a courtesy only. In the event that your interruptions impede this trial's progress, I won't hesitate to clear the courtroom.' He gazed sternly at one or two of the worse offenders in the audience, and the murmurs quickly died down. Satisfied, he gestured for the attorneys to approach the bench.

'Well, Miss Brevard, are you ready for your first criminal case?'

'I am, yes, Your Honor.'

Gail was already on edge. She had gone to the same courtroom where each *voir dire* had been heard, only to find that it was being used today for an entirely different case. The Powell trial, for some reason, had been moved to the top floor, and no one had notified her of the switch.

Redland asked pointedly, 'Do you still think your client is innocent, Gail?'

'I sure do . . . '

'We'll see what the jury says.'

'I'll beat you again, Turner, just like I did back in law school.'

The judge ignored the exchange and glanced out the window at the falling snow. 'If I forgot my tire chains, I'll have to send home for them before we adjourn for the day,' he muttered.

But Gail was staring pointedly at the blue-backed motion papers in the judge's hands.

West shrugged and turned to the Special Prosecutor. 'Well, Turner, what's on your mind here?'

'Your Honor, the People feel that former judge Zachary Ulrich, knew the deceased and knows the Seymour family intimately. For that reason, he might be an important witness.'

'If you want Zack Ulrich to testify I'm sure he'll do it, *after* you serve a subpoena.'

Gail spoke up without thinking. 'I'd be interested in questioning a witness like that myself.'

'But don't you see, Counselor?' Redland said, turning to her in triumph. 'Witnesses aren't permitted in the courtroom, as you well know, *only during the time they're testifying*.'

'This is a trick!' Furious, Gail turned to West. 'Turner will *never* call Zack to testify . . . and meanwhile the Defense will lose the benefit of his counsel and advice.'

West scraped a thin cheek thoughtfully. 'Well, Ms Brevard. I have to assume that the Special Prosecutor is acting in good faith, even though we're all aware that not every witness who is subpoenaed gets called to testify. I'll have to accept it, Counselor, under the circumstances.'

'I'll have the subpoena served immediately, Your Honor,' Turner Redland promised, smiling at Gail. 'Right now, in fact.'

* * *

While the matter of Zack Ulrich was being disposed of, Gail joined Damon. He was seated at the table in his dark blue suit, a white shirt and light blue tie. She had never seen him look more respectable. He had been slumped back in his chair, and now she gestured for him to straighten up.

A series of murmurs among the onlookers drew their attention, and Gail looked back to see Zack being shown out of the courtroom. The bailiff raised one hand disapprovingly at the talkers, and silence reigned once again.

'Are both sides actually ready?' the judge asked.

'The People are actually ready, Your Honor.'

'The Defense is actually ready.'

Damon's 'Not Guilty' plea was being entered by the clerk when Turner Redland slowly got to his feet, drawing the jury's attention.

'Your Honor, in the interest of saving time, the People will forego a preliminary statement of their case. The facts will be plain after the first witness has been questioned.'

It sounded good, but Redland had been making preliminary statements all through the *voir dire*, and hadn't thought twice about taking all the time he wanted — when he wasn't talking about the need to save time.

'The Defense will forego any statement at this time, but reserves the right to make one before we present our case,' Gail said.

Redland sniffed disapprovingly and turned toward the judge.

'The People will begin to lay the groundwork for their case,' he reiterated. 'The People call Officer Charles Hudson.'

The young policeman who had been instrumental in the capture of Damon Powell made his way to the stand and took the oath, looking around to make sure the court was full.

'Patrolman Hudson, how long have you been a member of the Cathcart police force?'

'June will be end of my third year.'

'Were you born in Cathcart?'

'I sure was. My girl friend, er, fiancée, is local, too.'

'During your time on the force, brief though it's been, have you won commendations?'

'Two times, sir.'

'Please tell the court why you were officially commended.'

'I saved three lives during a fire at the Seymour Mall.' Again he glanced around the courtroom. 'And I got a commendation for delivering a baby.'

'Did you say you were commended officially for saving several lives and for delivering a baby? Thank you. My hearing isn't always what it should be.'

Gail spoke under her breath. 'Your hearing will be fine when the defense is making points.'

Judge West interposed. 'I don't want any more stand-up comedy patter between Counsel. Questions about behavior will be directed solely to the bench.'

Gail said quietly, 'I beg the Court's pardon.'

Once again she had fallen head-on into another of the Special Prosecutor's traps, painting herself as someone who took petty advantage, and who would cheerfully commit the most dreaded sin of courtroom etiquette — that of wasting time.

Redland returned to the questioning.

'Now, Patrolman Hudson, directing your attention to the events of the night of November fifth last. Were you and your partner on duty in the Long Hills area of town?'

'Yes, sir.'

'Was this part of the regular route you are assigned to cover in your patrol car?'

'Yes, sir.'

'Did anything extraordinary happen on the night of November fifth?'

'It did.'

'Please tell the Court what transpired.'

'Trans . . . ?'

'What happened next?'

'I turned a corner and . . . '

'You were driving the patrol car?'

'That's right, sir. I turned a corner and there was someone in the headlights. Me and my partner got out and caught him — after he tried to run away.'

Judge West turned to Redland, 'Will the other officer be called to corroborate this testimony?'

'Yes, Your Honor, he will.'

'Proceed.'

'You were telling the Court, Officer Hudson, that you caught up with the intruder. Would that be the defendant, Damon Powell, seated over there?'

'It sure is, but he looked a lot rattier then.'

'Objection, Your Honor.'

'Sustained. The jury will disregard any characterization of the defendant as 'ratty,' by this witness.'

'Thank you, Your Honor,' Gail glanced pointedly at Damon, sitting up straight in his navy blue suit.

Turner continued: 'Your Honor, please ask the court stenographer to note that the witness has identified Damon Powell as the party he helped apprehend on the night of November fifth last.'

'So ordered. Proceed.'

'I would like to remind the Court that

Officer Hudson warned the young man that he and Officer Waghorn were members of the Cathcart police force, but that the defendant ran from them all the same. Is that so, Officer?'

'Sure is, sir. That's what the law tells us to do — and we do it — especially if it's dark and we can't be sure we can be seen by whoever we're stopping.' Hudson was more than a little annoyed that his adherence to the letter of the law would be questioned by anyone.

'All right, then, you caught hold of him, Patrolman Hudson. What happened next?'

'Actually Wag — Officer Waghorn — caught hold of him first, but between us, we held on to him.'

'Had any violence been offered against the defendant up until that time?'

'No, sir. None at all.'

'And I assume that you were suspicious of this defendant from the start?'

'People with nothing to hide don't run away from the police.'

'Objected to as a conclusion of the witness.'

'Then I'll have to take additional time to get the information in a different way,' Redland said, looking exasperated by Gail's tactics and glancing at the jury for sympathy. 'Well, did you notice anything about the defendant that made you consider the possibility that he might be lying?'

'Objected to for the same reason as before, Your Honor.'

'Very well then. After giving chase, you and your partner were not favorably disposed toward the defendant. I think that is a statement of fact which won't be disputed.'

'Yes, sir, it is.'

'We had better not try to use common sense, Officer, or my learned colleague here will be on my neck and we'll have to go into everything all over again and waste even more of our good time, not to mention keeping you from your job of helping to patrol Cathcart and keep order.'

Judge West said swiftly, 'I have warned the Special Prosecutor against making inflammatory remarks, and I will not tolerate a further breach of decorum from him in these precincts. One more lapse and a fine will be meted out.'

Redland sought sympathy from the jury for the second time and seemed satisfied by what he saw. Even when he went too far, it seemed, he still came out ahead.

'Take us through what happened next, Officer.'

'The guy didn't have any ID on him, but he said he had come from the Seymour house, that he was visiting them, so me and my partner took him to the house to check it out.'

'But before doing that, did you or your partner experience a different kind of difficulty with the defendant? Because of him, I mean?'

'Yes, sir. I suppose I should have said this before. Right where we were standing, I happened to kick something on the ground and it turned out to be a gun. It was an old-fashioned Colt .38 Special.'

'Did you know the caliber or make of the gun at that time? Then please discuss only what you knew while the events were taking place.'

'Yes, sir. The gun had been fired recently and me and my partner will swear to that in any court, in this world or the next.' Hudson looked warily over at Gail as if expecting her to contradict him. 'Then we took the suspect to . . . '

'One more moment, please, Officer Hudson. We are all anxious to hear what took place at the Seymour home, but I first want to ask whether any other discovery was made before you went there with the defendant.'

'Oh, yes, sir. We saw blood on the alleged perpetrator.'

'On his skin?'

'His clothes.'

'On his clothes, you say? Was there much blood?'

'About as big a stain as you'd get from two quarters. And believe me, one look at it and you knew it was blood. No mistaking it.'

'Was it wet?'

'Drying, I think.'

'You didn't touch it?'

'No, sir.'

'Then we had better keep to whatever

you know that is also beyond dispute.' Another quick look at the jury, silently reminding them that he had the attorney for the Defense to contend with — and thus must limit the type and style of questioning. 'At this time I have to ask if any violence was used by you or your partner against the defendant.'

'He caught a punch.'

'I beg pardon? You mean someone punched him? You or your partner?'

'It was me, sir.' Again that look around the courtroom. 'I had twisted an ankle on the gun, which had been thrown down on the ground, and I was mad and hurting. I shouldn't 'a done it, but a cop gets excited when he's hurt on the job by somebody like that, and things happen.'

Turner Redland faced the judge. 'The People will stipulate that in the heat of the moment a blow was struck in anger. The People don't believe that one blow affects the central issues of Patrolman Hudson's testimony.'

'The point is noted.'

'You and your partner then led the defendant to the Floyd Seymour home in the Long Hills section of Cathcart, Patrolman Hudson. Was the door of the house, the outside door, open or closed?'

'Closed but not locked, sir.'

'Tell the court what happened next.'

'Officer Waghorn, my partner, opened it and called out to ask if anyone was in earshot. There was no answer. We walked into the entryway and up a short flight of stairs into the living quarters. Vivian Seymour, the victim, was lying on the living room floor, dead.' There was a slight gasp from the onlookers. 'She had died, by violence, from person or persons unknown.'

'Would that be just an inference on your part?'

'No, sir. There was a lot of blood scattered on and about the body. There was no doubt in our minds, because of the position and condition of the body, that she was dead.'

'Surely the presence of blood wouldn't in and of itself be proof enough to permit a conclusion that Miss Seymour had died violently?'

'No, sir. But, you see she was lying on

the floor on her back. She'd been shot several times and her body looked like somebody had torn it apart — you know what I mean?' Officer Hudson fumbled to a halt.

'I'm afraid we all get the picture. The victim was undressed?'

'Yes, sir.'

The spectators murmured again and, once more, Judge West directed them to be quiet. At his signal, Redland continued.

'Let's recap. You, Officer Hudson, have stated that you and your partner, Officer Waghorn, came upon a young man loitering in the Long Hills neighborhood on the evening of November fifth last. A young man with blood on his clothing, who claimed to be acquainted with the Seymour family, and who appeared to have thrown away a handgun when you apprehended him after he gave flight. Upon further investigation, the body of a young female victim of violence, later identified as Vivian Seymour, was discovered by you and your partner in the living room of the Seymour home nearby. Do I have the details essentially correct?'

'Yes, sir. That's exactly what happened.'

Redland turned to Gail with a flourish. 'Yours.'

Gail took extra time to write down an added question that had occurred to her during Redland's examination. She looked levelly then at the youthful patrolman, and wondered how much his face would harden with the passage of time.

'Officer Hudson, you told the court about the commendations you've earned in only three years on the force.'

'And there were actually a couple of others I forgot to mention, but I'll be glad to do it now.'

Another small trap for her to fall into. 'I'm sure we can all feel better knowing that Cathcart's officers are so dedicated and hard-working.'

'Thank you, uh — Miss.'

'But I want the jury to decide if your brutality against the defendant was justified or is it merely a foreshadowing of the attitude that others have shown against this young man, *who is presumed innocent until proven guilty*, since the night of the crime.'

'I can't see . . . ,' Turner began.

But Gail skillfully overrode him. 'Officer Hudson. In your three years as a policeman, have you also been the target of any complaints about brutality or excess of force?'

Charles Hudson hesitated, obviously waiting for the *pro forma* objection from Redland, who immediately jumped to his feet.

'I realize that I opened the door for this question during my direct examination, Your Honor. But this officer has a job of some importance to the safety of our citizens, and the People don't feel that the Court's time should be wasted with this kind of frivolous diversion. All that matters is how he behaved on the night of November the fifth.'

Judge West looked annoyed at the Special Prosecutor. He was asking for support over an issue that could be brought up on appeal. 'Objection denied.'

To the witness he said bluntly, 'Answer the question.'

'Yes, ma'am, there has been a complaint.'

'Just one?'

'Two actually, but no more than that . . . '

'Excuse me, Officer Hudson. Did you say that there've been at least two complaints against you for brutality or exertion of force? Please speak up. The Special Prosecutor is sometimes hard of hearing — and I do want to make sure he hears you.'

Turner Redland pursed his lips in disgust at first then forced them into a semblance of a smile, facing the jury all the time to show that he could be a good sport when the tables were turned.

'Was either of those cases decided against you by your superiors?'

'One of 'em was. But the prisoner was a dope pusher, selling stuff to kids at my old school, and I would hit that piece of garbage again if I could. Pardon my language, Your Honor.'

'I might hit him, too, Officer. But I would be acting as a private citizen and you're a public servant. And because you have special duties and privileges, you aren't supposed to take advantage of your position to inflict harm on others. It's against the law. And by the way . . . Do you suppose those vigilante tactics of yours are what's kept you from being promoted?'

'Objection. The officer can have no knowledge of his superiors' reasons for their actions.' Turner tried to salvage the situation as best he could.

'Sustained.'

But Hudson had begun to speak too quickly. 'I have to take an exam and pass it before I can become a detective. I'm still workin' on that,' he added lamely.

Gail paused. In these first few minutes she had made a strong impression on the jury, she thought. Later, it would be more difficult to knock out any bad opinions of her that might yet be formed.

'Before you and your partner took the defendant into the Seymour house, the defendant 'caught a punch,' as you put it?'

'I admitted that.'

'Where did the punch land?'

'His stomach.'

'And before this punch was thrown, had the defendant offered any physical resistance?'

'He tried to run away.'

'But that doesn't involve a threat, Officer. Had the defendant made any menacing gestures toward you before that punch was thrown?'

'I didn't see none — any, I mean.'

'And had the defendant spoken any words that were in the nature of a threat to either you or to Officer Waghorn?'

'Nope. Not to me or to Jonas. No, he hadn't.'

'Had the defendant been informed he was under arrest?'

'Well, we didn't put him under arrest until just before we found the body.'

'But was he ever informed of his constitutional rights or warned against self-incrimination at any time?'

'Yes, ma'am. When we arrested him, he got warned.'

'But that was after you first saw him, and some time after you had apprehended him and subsequently punched him in the stomach, I suppose. Isn't that correct?'

'I suppose.' Hudson could see where this was going and kept looking longingly at Turner to release him from this purgatory.

'So about how long after . . . do you suppose?'

'Ten minutes, maybe. Twenty minutes tops.'

'So for as much as twenty minutes Damon Powell wasn't sure where he stood with you two. He couldn't possibly have called in a lawyer or anyone else to assist him in safeguarding his interests at a time when it was most crucial to him.'

Turner Redland rose. 'Objection. Where is the question in that?' He looked pointedly at the jury, silently apologizing for an inexperienced lawyer whose questions were so far out of line.

'Sustained. Continue, Counselor, with a question, not a statement.'

'Thank you, Your Honor. Now, Officer Hudson, I ask you to recall for us again your entrance into the Seymour home. In what order did the three of you proceed? Who came first, who came second, etc.?'

'Officer Waghorn led, the suspect was between us, and I brought up the rear. I had got hurt, you know, tripping over that gun of his, so I was limping a bit.' Hudson wanted everyone to remember about his injury in the line of duty.

'Thank you. Now, you and Officer Waghorn must have searched Damon Powell pretty thoroughly, once you got into the house and saw what had happened. Is that correct?'

'Yes. Me and Jonas ... Officer Waghorn ... wanted to be sure he wasn't carrying ... had another gun on him ... and we wanted to be sure he didn't have a knife hidden on him, either.'

'But you determined that he not only wasn't carrying a knife, but he did not have a gun on him either?'

'Well, he could 'a ditched anything he wanted to *before* we spotted him. Just like he got rid of the first gun.'

'Nevertheless, am I correct in stating that no weapons of *any* kind were ever found on Damon Powell's person? Answer yes or no, please.'

'No. We didn't find anything else.'

'Thank you, Officer Hudson. You've been very helpful.'

'Anything on redirect, Mr. Redland?'

Turner Redland stood at his table. 'Just one point, Your Honor. Given your years of experience on the force, Officer Hudson, did you see anything to indicate to you that the defendant might *not* be guilty?'

'What?'

'I'm asking you for your professional opinion about the defendant's guilt or innocence as you felt about it on the night in question.'

Gail decided against wasting time by making an objection. The jury certainly could guess what Hudson's answer would be.

'I didn't see or hear anything to give me the notion that Damon Powell might *not* be guilty.'

'I'm referring, you understand, to the defendant's attitude, his overall bearing when he was caught, and his responses to your questions. Does your answer still stand?'

'It does, sir.'

'Just a very few questions on recross, Your Honor,' Gail said smoothly. 'How many murderers have you been involved with in your three years on the force?'

'Maybe four or five. Murder doesn't

happen in Cathcart very often, thank God.'

'Thank God indeed. In any of those cases, was a suspect for the killing apprehended by you personally at the scene, or were you the arresting officer?'

'No.'

'And have you ever before been in the presence of an accused killer at the time of the discovery of the victim?' A dangerous question.

'Yes, ma'am, I have.'

'Briefly tell us the circumstances, not mentioning names or dates.'

'A wife killed her husband with a baseball bat, and we found her when she still had the bat in her hand. She looked frozen and numb, if you know what I mean.'

'Yes. Did Damon Powell look that way? Frozen and numb?'

'No, ma'am, he didn't.' Hudson had answered a little too quickly before thinking it through then looked disgusted when he realized what he had just said.

Gail stepped back to her place at the defense table. 'Nothing further for this witness, Your Honor.'

Turner Redland was on his feet after a

short pause. 'The People call Jonas Waghorn.'

The older officer climbed into the stand, gave his name and rank, took the oath, and then sank down into the chair. He stared wistfully at a ray of sun angled through the high-arched window, as if he wanted to follow that sunlight far, far away to some warmer and responsibility-free climate.

Redland began by leading him skillfully along much of the same ground through which he had taken Hudson, this time pressing for a more detailed description of the dead girl's appearance as he had found her.

The judge suddenly said, 'It's a bad follow-up to this kind of testimony, but we've reached time for our lunch recess.'

Gail swore under her breath at the notion of the jury members left with a recollection of violence described in detail, just before a two-hour lull.

Damon, however, smiled encouragingly at her while being taken away by the guard, oblivious of the various traps into which she had fallen.

9

At lunch, Zack listened impassively to Gail's report of the morning's session. When she was finished, he offered neither praise nor commiseration. Gail felt inclined to pay a little more attention to Zack's pronouncements, now that Turner had made it clear he didn't want the ex-judge in court. The fact was that Zack was making her a little tense. He hadn't taken well to Gail's suggestion of a working lunch near the courthouse. Inexplicably, he seemed concerned that her appearance in one of the local watering holes would look too much as if she was over-confident about the resolution of this case.

'So what does Johnny West think?'

'The judge? I honestly haven't a clue.'

'By this time, my dear, you should know everything he is thinking! If he's really against you, his rulings will be like poison.'

'There's always a chance he could change his mind when we make our case, though.'

'I doubt if he will. I'd say from experience that once he goes into a trial with his mind made up, he's not about to change it. Judges as a group aren't nearly as open-minded as lawyers might like to think they are. And they never like having to admit they've made a mistake.'

'All right then. You want to know what I think? He gives me the impression of bending over backwards to play right into Turner's game.'

'Now, that makes sense to me. You're probably right about that.'

'Then I'll have to turn him around somehow. I've got to make him change his mind.'

She was completely unprepared to see one of her firm's co-partners, Arnold Imlach, on his way out of the restaurant a few minutes later. He nodded and, after shaking hands with Zack, he smiled at Gail.

'So how is the big murder case coming along, young lady?'

'This is only the first day, sir, so I can't

really comment yet.'

'Is Johnny West treatin' you all right?'

'I'm hoping that he may see the possibility of my client's innocence.'

'More fool he if he does.' The old man's eyes narrowed at her coldly. Gail was shocked. Was he really that opposed to his firm's victory in this case?

Gail frowned at Zack when they were alone once more. 'I feel like I'm Alice down the rabbit hole!'

'And so you are, my dear. So you are.'

'I'll get the check, Zack,' she said as the waiter appeared. 'I haven't lost everything yet.'

★   ★   ★

'Thank you, Officer Waghorn,' Gail said at the end of her cross-examination. 'Nothing further.'

'And nothing on redirect.' But Turner went on to thank the weary witness for as much as a full minute, praising the deeds and accomplishments of the Cathcart police force for the benefit of the jury before he continued. 'The People call Dr.

Samuel Lefkowitz.'

The Cathcart Medical Examiner stepped forward and was sworn in. Turner rose and began the questioning. 'Vivian Seymour was shot three times, Doctor?'

'Yes. Once in the mouth, once in the chest . . . '

'And the third?'

The doctor hesitated. 'In the stomach area.' The onlookers gasped.

'You say that the third bullet struck Vivian Seymour in the stomach?'

'Objection. Asked and answered.'

'Sustained.' Judge West made a sound of near-disgust which no one in the jury could have failed to hear.

'Thank you, Doctor. Now, was it possible to ascertain which of the three bullets hit Vivian Seymour in the stomach region? In which order the bullets were fired?'

'No. That fact was impossible to ascertain.'

Gail moved her chair noisily and stood quickly.

'Can Counsel get on with the question-ing, if the Court please? A great issue has been made by him over the need to save time, and this particular juncture seems as good a place as any to prove his point.'

'That seems reasonable to me as well,' West said. 'Does the Special Prosecutor think he can move us forward?'

'I beg the Court's pardon,' Turner said, then resumed his questioning. 'Doctor, did you find any evidence that the victim attempted to fight off her killer before the shots were fired?'

'I found no evidence of that. There was no skin under the fingernails, for instance.'

'Doctor, I show you these photographs of the dead girl's body, which the People herewith introduce as People's Exhibit A and ask . . . '

Gail jumped to her feet. 'Your Honor, the Defense has not been given these photographs.'

'Come to the bench, please, both of you.'

West was carefully examining the photographs as Gail joined Turner. The judge's expression was sterner than usual as he perused the graphic evidence.

Without a word he passed the photographs over to Gail, who looked through them without comment until she came to two views near the end of the pile that showed the lifeless body of Vivian Seymour from head to bare feet.

'The Defense will object to these two being shown to the jury. They seem particularly inflammatory and add nothing to the information already provided by the others.'

The judge said, 'I suggest you rethink your objection.'

'Are you saying that you'd rule against my motion?'

'I am.'

Gail pursed her lips. If an argument could be made for the record, the question stood a chance of reversal on appeal. With the warning being given at the bench, though, any argument made for the record would run the added risk of antagonizing the judge even further. There was no longer any doubt what Judge West's opinion was concerning Damon Powell's innocence or guilt.

'Dr. Lefkowitz,' Gail said, when her

turn came. 'When you began your testimony, Mr. Redland spent quite awhile establishing your qualifications as a medical examiner, and the defense stipulated your qualifications subject to questioning at that time. Now, however, I would like to ask you in just how many criminal cases you have actually testified.'

Lefkowitz shrugged, 'Maybe four hundred, give or take.'

'You don't recall exactly?'

'Not to the exact figure, no.'

'If there were four hundred, there might be five hundred or six hundred.'

'Perfectly possible.'

'And that would include non-violent events, such as traffic deaths, for instance, where you might be called to testify at an inquest?'

'Yes. Of course.'

'And it's usually the city officials who call you in and for whom you testify?'

'My testimony is always neutral in tone, dealing only with the various causes of death, whatever that might be.'

'A simple answer of yes or no is sufficient, Doctor,' Gail said evenly. 'Now, directing your attention to the case before us. Can you estimate how far away the killer was from the victim when the lethal shots were fired?'

'About ten feet is my best estimate.'

'What makes you pick that distance?'

'The bullets left very few fuzzy edges on impact.'

'Had the victim engaged in sexual activity a short time before she was killed?'

'Because of the damage to that region, it is difficult to be positive but, in my opinion, she had.'

Turner rose. 'Is this line of questioning necessary? Haven't the girl's parents suffered enough without bringing in something that is entirely irrelevant as well as hurtful?'

'I'm inclined to give the Defense some latitude here,' West said. 'Subject to its being connected, of course.' But soon after making the statement, West ordered Gail and Turner back up to the bench, where he firmly emphasized that the matter of Vivian's morality, or lack thereof, should be downplayed. The judge then dismissed them, leaving Gail to get back to her cross-examination of the medical examiner. With not much leeway allowed, she eventually gave up and dismissed the doctor without further ado.

* * *

'The People call Ludlow Gates.' Gail consulted her notes on this particular witness with some concern.

The middle-aged man casually strolled up to the witness stand, took the required oath and sat down in the chair. He crossed his legs and folded his hands in his lap.

'You are an expert in the science of firearms identification?' Yeltoon asked.

'I am.' Gates's voice was as deep as if it was coming from the bottom of a well.

'You are experienced in identifying a gun fired during the commission of a crime?'

'That's correct.'

'And you have successfully identified bullets that may have been fired from such a weapon?'

'Yes, sir.'

'Please describe for the Court, in a general way, the procedure used for such an identification?'

'Every gun leaves distinct and unique markings on any bullet that is fired from it. You could say that every gun leaves its own unique image, sort of like a fingerprint.'

'How long have you been engaged in this type of work, Mr. Gates?'

'I've worked in this capacity for the State, off and on, for some eighteen years.'

'Now let us proceed to a discussion of the gun which was used in the murder of Vivian Seymour on the night of November fifth of this year.'

With the use of slides, Gates showed that, in his opinion, the three bullets fired into Vivian Seymour's body had all come from a Colt .38 Special which was now introduced as People's Exhibit B.

'Your demonstration was very clear, Mr. Gates,' Gail smiled as she got to her feet and stayed in place. 'I don't have any further questions for you at this time.' No point in staying on this topic any further. It won her nothing, and only reiterated facts she did not want to emphasize.

★   ★   ★

'The People call Shane Donahue.'

Donahue, a thin, nervous type, looked warily from left to right as he entered the witness box. He sat on the edge of his seat and in a low voice identified himself as a gun dealer by trade.

Turner, taking over from Yeltoon, asked, 'Do you recognize People's Exhibit B, Mr. Donahue?'

'Yes, sir. I was shown the gun by some of the District Attorney's people a little while ago.'

'Can you identify the make of the gun?'

'Yes, sir. It's a Colt .38 Special.'

'And have you had an opportunity to make a more detailed examination of this same weapon in the past?'

'I have, sir.'

'But how can you be sure about that? Counsel for the Defense is certain to ask, and we might as well get it straight between us now.'

'This particular gun has a little nick at the bottom of the barrel — see that? It's an x, actually.'

'Yes, I see it. I think that the jury will be interested in seeing it as well, Your Honor.'

Gail rose to her feet, but West cut her off with a wave of his hand. 'You haven't linked it up yet, Mr. Redland.'

'Very well, Your Honor. Now, Mr. Donahue. How did this x mark come to get to the bottom of the barrel? Can you tell us?'

'That mark was put on all his guns by a well-known collector of firearms. Following his death — the entire collection, including this gun, was purchased by me.'

'And you re-sold this particular Colt .38 Special? To whom?'

'To Mr. Burton Powell of this city, sir.'

'The defendant Damon Powell's father?'

'That would be the one. That's correct.'

'Do you know if Mr. Powell has a large gun collection?'

Gail spoke up. 'I don't see the importance of that.'

'If you care to make a formal objection, Counselor, I'll overrule. I admit to some curiosity about that fact myself.'

'Mr. Powell has purchased a few guns from me over the years,' Donahue continued smoothly. 'But my understanding is that his wife disapproves of keeping the collection in the house, so he has limited his purchases of late and has gotten rid of some of the items.'

'Do you know if Mr. Powell kept that particular Colt .38 Special?'

'He told me he was keeping it.'

'Had he asked you in the past about getting rid of other guns in his small collection?'

'Objection. Not material.'

'Overruled.'

'I'd like an exception on that, Your Honor.'

'Exception granted. You may answer the question, Mr. Donahue.'

'He had, sir, asked me about selling off some of his collection, that is.'

Turner Redland paused. 'Have I the Court's permission at this time to show the jury the murder weapon?'

Gail spoke. 'As I understand it, the jury is to examine the weapon for the sole purpose of confirming that a letter x is nicked under the barrel. Defense will stipulate the existence of the letter x under the gun barrel — solely in the interest of saving time, Your Honor.'

'And will the defense further stipulate that the gun in question belonged to Burton Powell, father of the defendant?' Turner pursued.

'So stipulated.' Gail tried to sound as if the matter was a minor issue. She needed to get out of this area quickly.

'In that case, Your Honor, the People waive the privilege of permitting the jury to examine the weapon at this time, subject to a renewed request if further testimony warrants it. Now, Mr. Donahue, are you acquainted personally with the defendant, Damon Powell?'

'Yes.'

'And when did you last see him? Do you recall?'

'During the last week of October.'

'And what was the occasion?'

'He came into my store to buy bullets

for that Colt .38 Special . . . '

'Objection. The witness could not know the bullets were purchased for that particular gun.' Gail jumped to her feet.

'Overruled. Proceed Mr. Redland.'

Turner resumed his questioning of Donahue, but Gail's interruptions had made it impossible to pick up the momentum again, and the gun dealer's subsequent evidence didn't appear to make a strong impression on the jury.

'I won't keep you long,' Gail said with a smile. 'I've only a few more questions. Was it unusual for Damon Powell to come into your store and buy ammunition for his father's guns?'

'No . . . '

'And, from time to time, do the relatives of other of your customers also come into your place of business and buy ammunition for family members?'

'Yes, some do.'

'Then Damon's actions or appearance did not seem unusual to you, nor did you suspect any plans for wrongdoing on his part?'

'No.'

'And did anything he said on that occasion make you suspicious?'

'No.'

'So nothing in his manner, his behavior, his attitude, or his language made you in any way think or believe that he might be up to no good?'

'Certainly not, or I wouldn't have given him the time of day, let alone sell him bullets for his father's guns!'

'Thank you very much, Mr. Donahue. You are excused.'

But Turner was already on his feet. 'Had the defendant ever before bought bullets for the Colt Special? In your recollection?'

'No. Not that I can remember. Usually he just bought ammunition for the hunting rifles.'

'But this particular time he bought bullets for the Colt Special?' Turner looked meaningfully at the jury. 'Thank you for making it clear to us, Mr. Donahue, and please accept my apologies for your having been delayed and needing to take time for this chore.'

Gail rose promptly. 'But still, there was

nothing whatever that could be called unusual in Damon Powell's manner or actions when he came to see you? Thank you very much, Mr. Donahue.'

The dealer stood up to leave the witness stand.

'Just one more point before I forget, Mr. Donahue,' she added, as if it was an afterthought. 'Have you talked about this case with opposing counsel? Has Mr. Redland helped you set up your testimony?'

Turner interrupted smoothly. 'There have certainly been discussions — two, I think — between Mr. Donahue and representatives of the People. But only to establish that he might have something to offer in evidence.'

'I asked for the witness's response, Your Honor,' Gail said sharply. 'Mr. Donahue, are you by any chance being paid directly or indirectly by the Special Prosecutor's office, or perchance by his representatives, to testify about this matter?'

'Absolutely not,' the gun dealer said firmly. 'Not one red cent has been paid to me!'

'And no *offer* of payment was made to you at any time?' Gail pressed.

'No, ma'am!'

'But has the city made any kind of an offer to buy guns from you when the police need new weapons?'

'Well, of course, it's understood that the police in any city generally buy from a local dealer.'

'And at present you're the only gun dealer of any size in Cathcart? Thank you very much, Mr. Donahue. Now you're excused.'

Redland said, 'Your Honor, it seems apparent that the Defense is trying to disguise the fact that it has no case, so instead Counsel is raising a fuss about a witness with perfectly valid testimony. These matters aren't substantive, and Defense knows it as well as anyone else.'

Gail sensed that the judge would snap at her if she allowed Turner to bait her any further, so she stayed quiet. But no judge could resist the temptation to appear as a peacemaker, a beacon of judicial sanity, and West was no exception. 'Step up here, both of you! Now it is my sincere desire that the two of you would stop bickering like a couple of schoolyard kids. Ms. Brevard, you are putting up one smokescreen after another, and I think there's a point past which the jury won't buy these obstructions of yours.'

'I'm simply doing my best to show the jury and the public what the mechanics of the prosecution's case are, Your Honor.'

'Well, you *should* be trying to help the proper administration of the law.' West paused as if he wanted that wise sidebar observation to be recorded somewhere. 'Now, how long is it going to take to put on the balance of this case? Both of you. Turner?'

'I should be finished by Monday morning — if all goes as planned.' He glared pointedly at Gail.

'My presentation should only take a day and a half,' Gail said.

'Well, get back to your pews, and I'll send this witness home before we adjourn for the day. Let's try and keep this civil, shall we?'

Gail took her seat as Donahue was thanked once more for his time and effort, by Judge West this time. He then turned to the jury. 'The jurors are hereby warned not to discuss the case among themselves or with outsiders and to report any attempt to influence their decision. I want to take a moment to commend you all for your diligence and attentiveness.'

10

'I feel like I'm jumping through hoops,' Gail said, leaning back.

'Are you too tired to talk?' Nick asked.

They were in the restaurant at Gail's hotel. The drapes at their table were partly open on a vivid full moon that shone down on drifts of snow which softened the faraway sounds of traffic in the street.

'If I were that tired I wouldn't be here in the first place,' she smiled.

'Whoa,' Nick said. 'I got the distinct impression that you were a shade too preoccupied to pay much attention to me.'

'Only for two seconds or so. I was just thinking how men are always so convinced they have some sort of godlike power over women.'

'Women have a lot of power of their own, if you want to know the truth. But must we argue about it?'

'But I'm a lawyer. I *like* to argue. It's my profession, after all!'

She didn't notice the frown cross his face as she took another sip of her drink.

'My uncle and aunt,' he began awkwardly, 'are suffering tremendously . . . '

'I'm sure they are, Nick. But that wouldn't be any different no matter what the circumstances were. If someone hadn't been put on trial and the murder remained unsolved, they would still be suffering.'

'And if Viv had died from natural causes, they still would suffer, of course,' he agreed. 'You'll get no argument there. But as it is, they're very hurt, in agony even. For the first time I can remember, they simply don't know which way to turn.'

'I can understand that. A tragedy in the family can be — hard, very hard, especially when it seems so senseless, as this one does.' Self-absorbed as he was at the moment, he hadn't caught the sad undertone in Gail's usually cheery voice.

'They expect me to be closer to them than I have been since I moved out to San Francisco,' he went on. 'And in that way, I

181

suppose, I provide some sort of solace as the son who survived.'

'That's a lot to put on you.'

'Oh yes, it's all of that. Nobody lives without pain and very few of us die without it.'

'My actions in court aren't meant to add to their pain needlessly, Nick. What I have to do is prove that the police have got the wrong man so I can win an acquittal for my client.'

'So you still believe he's innocent?'

'The police haven't proved a thing. Look, Nick. I have no idea what actually happened that night, but I think there's a very real possibility he didn't do it. I'm not trying to play God here. I'm bound by the law, and my own conscience, to do everything I can to put my best case forward for my client and let the jury do its duty in turn to make a decision that will sit well with the rule of law and common sense. That's my assignment, and I intend to fulfill it.'

'It sounds like you enjoy playing the game and are determined to win at all costs.'

'What are you really trying to say, Nick?'

'You've been assigned to get this vermin acquitted, to be the heroine who gets him off. You feel that his future is in your hands and no one else's, and that gives you a thrill, doesn't it? It gives you a sense of power to have a human life depending on you . . . '

'You know something, Nick? It must be wonderful to know what somebody else is *really* like, especially a woman — am I right?'

'No, that isn't right — or fair. If you want to think that I'm convinced you're doing this because you see it as a chance to shine in a man's arena, well, that's up to you. But it's not what I meant.'

'Well, whatever you meant, I think you'd better make yourself clear — before I lose all interest in this little charade!'

'I think you've found a new and fascinating game, Gail. And you're going to play it as well as you can. The game is for you to win, just as a man might put that ball on the enemy's goal line, hit a home run, sink a basket. But those situations don't call for moral choices and this one does.'

'I'm doing the job I've been assigned to do, to the best of my ability . . . and I believe I'm doing it ethically and morally.'

'And you're caught up in the glory of the game, of winning, and you don't care that you're trying to set a monster loose on society, a monster who has killed at least once and might very well do it again.'

'Nick! It's not my job to assume he's guilty. My job is to do the best for my client that I possibly can. No matter how hard the officials in high places try to stop me. I have to present my client's case in the best possible light and let the jury make the final decision.'

'But your skills could influence the jury unduly, and a killer would be free as air.'

They were repeating themselves she knew, but she couldn't resist the need to win this one argument, even though she knew she would never win.

'So you're telling me that I should put up only a minimum defense to the prosecution and make no attempt to defend my client to the best of my ability — all because you happen to believe he is guilty?'

'I think you should act like the officer of the court you are and do your best to make sure justice is upheld.'

'At least I've never tried to take an undue advantage in influencing that person.'

'Gail! That's so unfair!'

'Is it?' She reached for her coat. 'Don't call me, Nick. I'll call you when I'm good and ready, not before.'

He looked away. '*Fini la commedia* — isn't that it?'

''Fraid so, Nick. Believe me, it's better this way,' she said, then added quietly, 'I'll miss you though, for whatever the hell that's worth!'

She went quickly out of the restaurant before he could respond and moved silently down the hall to the elevator. She entered her suite on the floor above, ordered a drink from room service then went to bed. She slept soundly for a full eight hours and, remarkably, her dreams were no more intense than usual.

John West usually went one night a week to his private club in town to take advantage of the gym and sauna. He then spent the balance of the evening playing cards with a group of long-time cronies.

As the judge left the sauna this night on his way to the game, he was confronted by Oliver Kincaid, the founder and CEO of a flourishing company, and a member of the influential social set in the Cathcart area.

'Come into the lounge a moment, John, if you don't mind.'

'Can this wait?' West was impatient to get to the game.

'I don't think so.'

The comfortable dimly-lit lounge was dotted with groups of upholstered chairs placed intimately for the optimum in private conversation. A bar at one end of the room featured a big-screen TV, set to one of the sports channels. A fireplace on another wall leant a subtle warmth to the ambience. The two old friends found a quiet spot and ordered drinks. West leaned back and eyed Kincaid cautiously.

'What's up, Ollie?'

'I'm wondering what your take is on that murder case you're hearing, John. You know, that kid . . . ?'

'Damon Powell?' West hesitated. 'What do you mean, 'What's my take on it?''

'A lot of us in town, Floyd and Nancy's friends, don't think they should be asked to testify. Shouldn't be put through any more of this . . . You know what I'm saying, John . . . '

'Look. I care about them, too — so does Turner. He's looking to move up the ladder, so he's not likely to rock any boats here.'

'But that girl of Morin's? Would she?'

'I doubt it. The Seymours are the victims here. She's not going to want to put them on the stand and risk diverting sympathy away from her client.'

'But I understand she questioned Floyd before the trial . . . ?'

'Oh that! That was standard procedure, Ollie. She got nothing from that.'

Kincaid paused, gazed into the fire and sipped his drink.

'Johnny. Do you know if she'd be likely to call anyone else like that to testify?'

'Who do you have in mind, Ollie? Come out with whatever it is that's bothering you . . .'

'All right, then. Do you think she might call Laura?'

West paused. 'I doubt Gail Brevard *knows* your daughter. Why should she? Unless you've crossed paths with her somehow . . . ?'

'I hope you're right about that,' Kincaid said. 'But suppose she hears gossip from some girl who's jealous of Laura. Someone who would be prepared to say she knew Powell. What then?'

'Gossip isn't evidence, Ollie. It's hearsay. You know that.' West was getting bored with this conversation and stood, stretching his back to the fire.

'Did you know she's hired the Goldthwaites?'

'So what? I can't see what difference that makes.'

'I suppose you're right . . .'

'One hand still washes the other, my boy. If the Goldthwaites and Ms. Brevard want to 'get along' in this town, then they had better 'go along.''

'It still bothers me that she seems to be fighting tooth and nail to get that murderer off.'

'I'll admit that no one expected her to be even minimally effective.' West shook his head. 'She's purely a corporation attorney, and I'm sure Randy believed that after she started this trial under pressure, she'd sink without a trace. But she's a fighter, that one, and it's been a dust up between her and Turner from the get-go.'

'Sounds to me like Powell's convinced her he's innocent.'

'That may be, but Gail Brevard doesn't strike me as being naïve . . . '

'It's my understanding that the little snake is persuasive,' Kinkaid said, interrupting West. 'He's one of those kids who knows just what it takes to persuade a girl . . . any girl. They feel sorry for him, ya' see, and before they know it they're eating out of his hand.'

West kept his own counsel.

'Laura knew him just slightly, that's all,' Kincaid added unnecessarily.

'All I can tell you, Ollie,' West reiterated, 'is that what you fear most isn't going to happen. Laura will not be asked to testify. Neither, in my opinion, will the Seymours, for that matter.'

Kincaid looked coolly at the judge. 'Can you promise that?'

'I'll see to it if I must.'

Kincaid drew a deep breath as West looked at his watch once again.

'Thanks, Johnny. You've taken quite a load off my mind.'

'Yes, I can see that. Look, I've got to meet some of the boys for our weekly get-together. Care to join us?'

'No thanks, John. I'll take a rain check.' Kincaid rose, shook West's hand then made his way to the front of the club. The Judge stood a moment longer looking after him, deep in thought, then shrugged and turned away. It wasn't his problem . . . and he intended to keep it that way.

* * *

West didn't feel the slightest hesitation in speaking bluntly to Zack Ulrich.

'How's the Powell case seem to you? Ms. Brevard doing all right there?'

'You know as much as I do,' Zack said. 'I'm not as much in her confidence as I was at first. Some of my suggestions proved to be way too helpful to Turner, and that woman has a memory like an elephant!'

'But is she still talking to you about the case?'

'Off and on. Sure. But she isn't accepting my advice the way she was before, without mulling it all over and making up her own mind about it. She's a smart cookie, too. Fool her once, shame on you . . . You get the picture.'

'Has she said anything at all about Ollie Kincaid's daughter, Laura?'

'Funny you should mention that. She's dead certain that Laura not only knows Powell, but that they are very close. Odd, that, considering he was apparently seeing the Seymour girl as well.'

'But do you think she's crazy enough to call Laura to testify?'

'I doubt it, John. She's already thought that one over and couldn't see any advantage to her client with that. But Johnny, I can't be sure what she's going to do. She still gives me a few scraps, but she's playing things pretty close to the chest these days.'

'But if she gets desperate and has nowhere else to go, do you think she would pull such a stunt? Put Laura Kincaid on the stand, I mean. What's your honest take on that?'

'She can't be sure how much a jumpy teenager might give away on the stand and, in my opinion she's smart enough to realize how dangerous that could be. You know the old adage, never ask a question if you don't already know the answer . . . '

'Well, try to stay in the loop with her. Hold her hand if you must. We can't afford any loose cannons here. Ollie's jumpy enough as it is. Don't want *him* going off the deep end'

'I'll do what I can. But, to be perfectly frank, I can't make you any promises.'

'Your best is good enough for me, Zack. As always . . . '

The two old friends closed their conversation with some lighter discussion about an upcoming card game. But John West had a frown on his face when he hung up. Would this case just go away!

★ ★ ★

Buried deep in snow, the Long Hills community presented a cheery holiday façade to the passing parade. The lovely old mansions resembled gingerbread houses, scattered here and there on a counterpane of white, lights aglow, wisps of smoke rising from each chimney, and the ubiquitous sparkling Christmas tree in each and every front window.

Oliver Kincaid parked his Mercedes slightly askew in the front drive and stared out at the wintry landscape with the slightly nauseous sensation that he had landed in the midst of a Grandma Moses painting. He made his way gingerly up an icy pebbled path between twin wooden terraces lined with lighted miniature cedars. The house itself was a sturdy-looking brick structure partially fronted by a long overhang punctuated with *faux* marble columns. Reaching the entrance, he entered numbers into an alarm pad. There was a discrete click and the door opened wide to his touch.

The sound of crying came from the living room off the entry. Kincaid headed for the comfy space with its pitched roof and center skylight where he stopped, a frown lining his brow.

Anna Kincaid was standing with a forefinger extended threateningly, her face creased, like her husband's, but in anger. Their daughter, Laura, was sprawled carelessly across the arm of a nearby chair. She had her father's handsome features combined with her mother's slender build. Pale white hands that had never seen dishwater covered her face.

'I'll keep you home if I must,' Anna Kincaid said. 'The University will just have to get along without you.'

Laura dropped both hands from her reddened face. She wavered between gasping for breath and sobbing anew.

Anna turned to her husband in exasperation. 'This has been going on forever, but you'd rather be out gallivanting around with your pals than stay home and support me here. No wonder I've been forced to take a prescription just in order to get some sleep. This is all your fault!'

He started to tell her that he had talked to John West, just as they had agreed he must, and that the judge had been most encouraging. But he didn't think it was wise to bring up the topic in front of Laura, so for the moment he stood there quietly and let her abuse roll off him. Successful as he was in dealing with colleagues, he couldn't seem to get a handle on these highly emotional moments at home. It was easier by far just to leave it to his wife to try to keep their high-strung daughter in line.

Laura, for her part, continued her argument. 'But I *love* him — and he loves me! And I *should* testify for him. He just *couldn't* have had anything to do with that Vivian Seymour — Damon loves *me*!'

Anna Kincaid lashed out, '*Nothing* you could possibly say in court would be of the slightest help to that — that despicable person!'

Oliver looked longingly toward the kitchen. 'I think I'll get some coffee . . . '

No one heard him. 'At his age, a boy can claim he loves one girl — and even believe it — then turn around and go off with another one whenever he wants,' Anna persisted. 'Believe me, I know what I'm talking about . . . '

'You're just saying that 'cause you're jealous of me! You're like all the rest of those hypocrites — !' Laura hiccupped a stifled sob.

Anna took this opportunity to direct a long angry glance at her husband. 'If you weren't away all the time,' she said accusingly, 'doing whatever, you'd be here to help me while I'm trying to deal with this nonsense day and night.'

He blew up. 'And if you weren't taking all those pills to knock you out all the time, you'd be better able to deal with these issues!'

'And you're such a great help! Go on. Have your coffee. Run away, like you always do.'

Her accusation stung but, in spite himself, he shrugged and headed out to the kitchen where indeed, he caught himself dawdling over the exact amount of creamer to add to his coffee. He returned to the battleground slowly — balancing the cup carefully, to keep from spilling it — and once again heard his wife cry out.

'Laura, don't you understand you can't help Damon — no matter what you might say or do? He'll be punished for his crime. No doubt about it. And you'd be punished as well, by all the powers that be. You might as well forget marrying someone nice and having a decent life here.'

'I don't care!'

'Oh yes you do!' Anna said in triumph. 'You know you need the good things in life as much as I do. You'd give up a lot for the good things, just as I would — and have in my life.' She eyed Oliver narrowly. 'Now you can just shut up about all that!'

Laura fell silent. But a resentful pout played about her full lips. She would be quiet, for now. But she hadn't surrendered. Not by a long shot . . .

'Now I want your word, Laura, that

you won't try to help that — that despicable creature in any way.' Anna, assuming she had won the skirmish, persisted.

'I won't promise! Never! I'll never promise you anything!'

'In that case, we're all going to have the longest argument in recorded history, because I won't let you out of my sight until this idiotic trial is over with. Is that clear?'

Silence.

'I'll consider that to mean that you've given me your word. Now go to your room. I'm sick of all this.'

Laura eyed her father as she sidled off to her room. She knew she had won, but the whole thing had set her to thinking again. She understood (or thought she did), why Damon was keeping her out of the picture as an alibi. Either he had been ordered not to mention her, or he had figured out on his own that it would be a mistake to turn people like her father against him. It wouldn't help his case if he was targeted as a nobody wannabe who had the nerve to go after one of the elite. If she had to stake her life on it, she would have said someone had gotten to him.

Thinking about all this, not to mention the knockdown, dragout with her mother, had given her a humungous headache. She was sure she wouldn't be able to fall asleep on her own. Better sneak one of mom's pills for herself. She'd done it often enough before. Anna Kincaid never seemed to keep track of them or realize any were missing.

Pensively Laura undid the top button of her blouse and touched the pendant she wore next to her skin before climbing into bed, where she quickly sank into a deep dreamless sleep.

11

'The People call Sergeant Arthur Rolfe,' Turner Redland said.

It was a quarter past two, and the trial had resumed following lunch. Damon stared a little wistfully out at a mountain of recent snow, which had already turned to grayish slush. Gail touched his hand in silent support.

She recalled the bullish Rolfe from their brief exchange back at Police Central during her first hours on the case and how adamant he was concerning Damon's guilt. She wasn't surprised then, when under Redland's skillful questioning, the sergeant recounted the conclusions he had drawn about the case, when he was put in charge of the detail called to the Seymour home the night Vivian's body was discovered. This testimony wasn't of any real value to his case, but Turner obviously wanted to keep hammering home to the jury the gory details of the brutal killing.

Gail began her cross-examination slowly.

'Sergeant Rolfe, you've told the court that you were in charge of the officers who examined the house after the murder. I assume that among them were forensics specialists?'

'Yes, ma'am.'

'And what were the specialties of those police personnel?'

'There was a fingerprint specialist, the police photographer, two EMTs, of course, for transporting the body to the morgue, and a few other police officers.'

'Did any of these specialists find even the slightest evidence linking the defendant, Damon Powell, to the crime in question?'

'Not specifically. Not as far as I am aware of.'

'But you *would* be aware of it, wouldn't you? Wouldn't all this have been discussed, perhaps more than once, between you and your superiors?'

'I suppose so. Since the defendant was the only one found at the scene, it seemed to be a foregone conclusion. That he was the guilty party, I mean.'

'Then the answer is that, to your

knowledge, no one in this 'cast of thousands' found any significant evidence at all linking my client, Damon Powell, to the murder of Vivian Seymour?'

Turner shot to his feet. 'Objection! I don't see any need to have this witness and the efforts of the entire police department denigrated like this!'

West cleared his throat. 'Watch it, please, Ms. Brevard.'

'Thank you, Your Honor. Now, Sergeant Rolfe. To your knowledge, was any evidence found on the scene which incriminated anyone else?'

'No. Absolutely not.'

'And, again to your knowledge, was a thorough search made of Miss Seymour's private possessions? I'm speaking now of the sort of thing that a young girl might keep hidden, or out of sight, such as a diary, or journal? That kind of thing?'

Rolfe looked a little uncomfortable. 'I didn't myself, but I suppose there was bound to be some of that. I couldn't really say . . . '

'You don't know if any of the victim's possessions were examined for clues

— even though, supposedly, you were in charge of the investigation?'

'I like to give my people discretion to follow their own judgment in such matters. Besides, we had the perp — the alleged perpetrator in custody. There didn't seem to be no point to disturbing the house any further . . . ' He glanced at Turner in some dismay.

'So your people did whatever they wanted to do in terms of securing the crime scene?'

'I didn't mean it quite like that.'

'Let's move on to another aspect of the search, Sergeant. Did your forensics specialists find fingerprints other than those belonging to the family?'

'Oh yes, plenty. There were fingerprints all over the place . . . '

'But none, I take it, belonging to Damon Powell? If you believed him to be the perpetrator of the crime, then he must have been in the room where the murder took place — and by standard rules of deduction, he should have left his fingerprints there. That is, unless he was wearing gloves. Was he wearing gloves when apprehended? No? Then did your forensics specialists find any gloves at the scene, which appeared to belong to the defendant? No? Doesn't that strike you as a little surprising, Sergeant? Particularly when he was apprehended right there, as you say, at the scene? He would hardly have had time to dispose of the gloves, if he was, indeed, wearing them . . . '

Turner snapped, 'He's trying to give you what he has, so don't make a Federal case out of it!'

Judge West intervened. 'The Defense's statement was out of line, I agree, but the Prosecution needs to watch its implications as well. I've previously warned the two of you not to engage in such tactics, and I don't intend to do it again. Proceed, Ms. Brevard, with caution.'

'I beg the Court's pardon,' she said. 'But there are pictures of the entire living room as it looked at the time the body was discovered, and those pictures have not been put into evidence as yet. I now ask that it might be done.'

Turner quickly responded. 'I'm sorry, Your Honor. The pictures Counsel refers to will now be offered as People's Exhibit C.' She wondered if Turner was on the level for once, or secretly reveling in yet another opportunity to emphasize the carnage once again. Either way, she felt she had at least gotten her point across about the evidence, or lack of it. After reviewing a few more salient points she wanted to make about the room for the jury, she returned to her seat and waited for the next act.

'Call your next witness, Mr. Redland,' West said. 'Let's move on.'

★   ★   ★

'The People call Dr. Anthony Colbert.'

Looking every bit as dapper as he had at the bail hearing, the psychiatrist walked to the stand and took the oath.

Turner caught Gail off guard by not reiterating Colbert's sterling medical and psychiatric qualifications, but launched instead directly into the questioning. Had he forgotten such an obvious introduction, or did he have another trick up his sleeve?

'Dr. Colbert. Were you at Police Central after midnight on the night of November fifth last?'

'I was.'

'And did you have an occasion to see the defendant at that time?'

'I not only saw him, but I heard him as well. I'm sorry to say I wasn't permitted to examine him in detail, though.'

'And how was the defendant dressed at that time?'

'Objection, Your Honor. What Damon Powell was or was not wearing is irrelevant.'

'Sustained,' Judge West agreed. 'Move on.'

'What did the defendant say within your hearing?'

'Objection! Hearsay.'

'There's no need for this nitpicking here, Your Honor,' Turner replied. 'It wastes the Court's time. Your Honor, the People will link this testimony.'

'If it please the Court, this witness is being asked to repeat what the defendant may or may not have said before he was allowed contact with an attorney. His behavior at that time can have no bearing on the record.'

'But it does go to demeanor, Your Honor. The jury is entitled to know what the defendant was saying and doing at that time of his arrest. And Dr. Colbert is an expert in such matters.'

'If you can link it up, Mr. Redland, I'll allow it,' West said.

'An exception, if the Court please.'

'So noted, Ms. Brevard. Now, Mr. Redland, let's move ahead.'

The stenographer read the last question back. Colbert paused then stated: 'The defendant cursed steadily, nearly the whole time I was with him.'

'Was there any object to his cursing? Did he mention any one or any thing specifically?'

'Well, he was cursing the police, in part, for arresting him in the first place. Mostly, though, he was cursing the dead girl, Vivian Seymour.' There was a ripple of sound and movement across the courtroom, causing West to glare warningly at the onlookers.

'He cursed Vivian Seymour, knowing

she was the victim of such a horrible death?' Turner looked about in disbelief. 'What on earth did he say about her?'

'Objection, Your Honor. I really must protest this deliberately inflammatory discussion . . . '

'Overruled.'

'Exception again, Your Honor.'

'Granted. Continue . . . '

'Dr. Colbert? If you can recall . . . ?'

'The defendant used most of the usual epithets. Is it necessary for me to repeat them here?'

'I feel I'm obliged to ask for an example, Dr. Colbert. My apologies.'

Colbert sighed and began again. 'Damon Powell called Vivian Seymour a . . . '

Judge West made Gail's objection for her this time. 'We've taken this far enough now, Mr. Redland. Please move on.'

Turner Redland stood triumphant, with feet apart and hands behind his back, like the captain of a ship in the teeth of a gale. 'I regret sullying this courtroom with such filth, Your Honor, but the People consider it relevant to illustrate both the defendant's attitude toward the murdered girl and his state of mind shortly after the crime had been committed.'

'Very well. You've made your point. Please move on to something else.'

But Turner had done enough damage. He gestured toward Gail. 'Yours,' he said, with a touch of irony in his voice.

Gail figured he expected her to ask why Dr. Colbert had been at Police Central that night, which would then open up the whole line of testimony about the man's extensive professional background, thus lending credence to all he had said. She was beginning to catch on to Turner's tricks.

'No further questions for this witness,' she said and sat back down.

Turner's head shot back in anger. Now he would be forced to do what he had expected her to do for him.

'Your Honor, the People ask that the Court permit a redirect examination of this witness.'

'By precedent, Mr. Redland, you know you can't hold a redirect examination if cross examination has been waived.'

'Then may I be permitted to add to my

examination-in-chief, if the Court please?'

'The Defense will object, Your Honor, on the grounds that the Special Prosecutor has made it clear that his examination-in-chief is concluded.'

'Mr. Redland?'

Turner pursed his lips, but didn't pursue the matter. 'Your Honor, at this time the People wish to make an offer of proof in the matter of the testimony of Dr. Colbert.'

'Very well,' Judge West nodded. 'The jury will be escorted out while the proof is read into the record.'

Turner spoke quietly and quickly, adding into the record an extensive list of Dr. Anthony Colbert's educational achievements and psychiatric training, his field experience, the number of articles on criminal behavior which he had had published, in short, all of his qualifications as an expert witness. Once the record was complete, the jurors made their way back in slowly, most looking resentful at having been left out of the loop in this manner. The Judge explained it all to them.

'The Special Prosecutor, Mr. Redland,

has put into the record a number of matters to which one of his witnesses would have testified under oath. It doesn't follow that the testimony would have been accepted by you or that the Defense might not have objected to it on some level. That is something I must make clear. Mr. Redland, by making what is called an 'offer of proof,' has merely followed one of the many technical procedures which the law mandates in case this matter is heard in time by a higher court.' Most of the jurors looked even more confused at this explanation and shifted uncomfortably in their seats.

West glanced impassively over at Redland, who was trying his best to look self-assured and as if he was in control of the situation. 'Now, Mr. Special Prosecutor, may we please have your next witness?'

* * *

'The People call Chad Wilson.'

A big man emerged from the little room off to one side. When he settled down, he looked as if he had been squeezed so tightly into the huge chair that he couldn't have made another move to save his life.

'Your name is Chad Wilson and you are the official photographer for the Cathcart Police Department?'

'Yes, sir. I am.'

'And in that capacity, you were sent to the Seymour home in Long Hills on the night of November fifth last?'

'Yes, sir.'

'And there you took photographs of the dead girl and the room in which she was butchered?'

'Objection, Your Honor. The word 'butchered' is unnecessarily inflammatory.'

'Sustained.'

'I apologize, Your Honor. Mr. Wilson, you took official police photographs of the crime scene as it was discovered in the Seymour home?'

'I did.'

'Do you refer to these photographs that have already been put into evidence as Peoples Exhibit C?'

'Yes, sir. These are the photographs I took at the Seymour home.'

Gail stood. 'May I ask how many pictures were taken altogether, Mr. Wilson?'

'About twenty-five, I believe.'

'But how many of the twenty-five or so photographs you took have been offered today here in evidence?'

'Six or eight, I think. Some didn't come out and some others just weren't clear,'

'Nevertheless, Defense asks to have *all* of the pictures you took at the Seymour house on November fifth last offered into evidence, Your Honor.'

Turner Redland looked incredulous. He wavered between standing to object, then thought better of it and stayed quiet.

'So ordered,' Judge West said.

Damon turned to her as she took her seat: 'They seem to be glad you put those pictures in so they can be shown to the jury. What's your idea?'

'My idea is that the jury will get bored with all that detail and won't hesitate so much over each and every photograph. I'd rather get them to a point where they look away and shrug rather than ooh and ah over each one.'

'That's pretty smart,' Damon decided. 'I knew you'd knock them for a loop!'

Gail felt a tap on her shoulder and whirled around. One of the bailiffs was leaning over to offer an envelope with a note: 'Talk to me before you question the next witness. H.G.'

'Your Honor,' Gail said, 'at this time the Defense requests a ten minute recess to confer with a colleague.'

'Granted. The jurors will remain in their seats.'

'I can tell you something about the next witness,' Hugo said before she could ask. 'It's a relative of the Seymours being brought in to establish that the family is shaken and is anxious to have closure in this matter.'

'Nick Quintaine, is that right?' Why was Hugo telling her this? There wasn't a thing she could do about it, and this testimony wasn't likely to make much difference anyway.

'How did you? — never mind.' He paused. 'The case isn't going too badly for you, you know, considering how strong the evidence is against the kid.'

'So far, so good,' Gail admitted grudgingly.

'Will you be putting him on the stand?'

'Damon?' Gail wondered why Hugo wanted to know. 'I haven't decided, yet.'

'Nobody knows better what actually happened that night.'

Gail looked at the investigator thoughtfully. 'What I really need is an extra day to coach him — *if* I decide to put him on the stand, that is,' she added quickly. She wished she could tell Hugo to go back and let whoever was paying him know that she was on to their game. But it was far better to let him — and everyone connected with him — believe she didn't understand what was really going on.

★   ★   ★

Moments later she returned to the defense table as Nicholas Quintaine was called to the stand.

'You are related to the Seymours? How, if I might ask?'

Nick replied with a brief explanation and the questioning continued smoothly. Nick made it clear how devastated the Seymours were over the senseless tragedy that had befallen their only child — and he added that he, himself, had never heard anything derogatory about Vivian.

'Yours,' said Turner curtly.

Gail waited until Nick's eyes met hers. There were a dozen questions she could ask, but every one would only prove again that even wealthy and influential parents like the Seymours could grieve deeply over a young daughter's senseless murder. Prolonging this line of questioning would almost certainly gain the jury's sympathy against her client. The only thing she would accomplish would be to convince them even further that she neither understood nor cared about the human tragedy that had taken place.

'Mr. Quintaine,' she said. 'You and the Seymour family have my deepest sympathy for your loss. I hope you'll convey my sincere feelings to your aunt and uncle.'

Nick nodded, but said nothing.

'Your Honor, I have no questions of

this witness at this time.'

'Do you have anything further for this witness, Mr. Redland?'

'No, Your Honor, and in the interest of saving as much time as we may be allowed to, the People are pleased to be resting our case, thus sparing the Court and the jury from unnecessary repetition of the facts already established.'

West glanced at his watch. There was enough time before the scheduled recess for Gail to enter the Defense's inevitable motion for a D.A. — a directed acquittal — on the grounds of insufficient evidence — and time enough for him to turn it down. The jury would then mull over that negative opinion during the entire two-hour lunch break.

'Well, it isn't quite time for recess yet, Counselor,' the judge said pointedly to Gail. 'If you have any motion to make, do it now.'

'Sidebar, Your Honor?'

'Come, both of you.' West gestured. 'But don't take all day about it, Ms. Brevard. Make your motion now — or be done with it.'

'I'm prepared to make my motion and have it accepted . . . '

'Very funny!'

' . . . or rejected on its merit . . . but only when the trial resumes after lunch. You see, I'd have to refer to *so many* precedents pertaining to a possible rejection, that the jury may become quite impatient and irritated with *everyone* who is preventing them from taking their lunch break.' She smiled sweetly at the pair of them.

'All right,' West conceded, to Redland's obvious disgust. 'You win. We'll take our lunch first.'

12

For some reason Gail relished her lunch more than usual at the *Third Call* that day. But trying to elicit information from Zack without giving away anything in return, was no easy task.

After jousting with Zack for the better part of an hour, Gail found herself back on the street and headed toward her hotel to freshen up and review her notes. Suddenly she was waylaid by a woman who gave off an undeniable aura of privilege and wealth.

'You're Ms. Brevard . . . that despicable boy's lawyer!' the woman said. 'I was certain I recognized you. I need to speak with you. At once.'

'Are you a reporter? If so, I have no comment . . . '

The woman shook her head impatiently. 'No. Of course I'm not a reporter. You *must* come with me,' she insisted.

'Come with you? Why? Where?' Gail

looked around for Zack, or Hugo, or anyone else she knew to assist her with this predicament.

But the stranger only frowned and pointed imperiously towards an expensive car parked nearby.

'I'm sorry.' Gail insisted. 'But I have a long list of things I must take care of right now. Then I'm due back in court this afternoon. I can't come with you right now.'

'John West will wait for you.'

'Judge West? Not for me he won't!'

But just as Gail was about to make her departure, Randolph Morin, turned the corner on his way in to the *Third Call*. He glanced quizzically from Gail to the unknown woman, then smiled genially at them both and nodded a welcome.

'Well hello, Anna. I hope everything's all right with you. I spoke with Ollie the other day . . . I didn't realize you were acquainted with Gail?' He looked questioningly at his junior associate.

'Yes, thank you, Randy, I — we're all fine.' She was obviously a little uncomfortable at being caught this way, but

Morin didn't seem aware of it. He spoke a few more words to the both of them before turning to make his way into the restaurant.

Gail had been looking intently at the woman. 'I've seen you somewhere before, but I'm afraid I can't put a name to it,' she said finally.

'I'm Anna Kincaid,' the intruder said simply. Of course! Oliver Kincaid's wife! Laura Kincaid's mother! Gail kicked herself for not having recognized the woman immediately. She quickly made a decision. 'Look, I really can't take the time to come with you right now . . . but I can meet with you later this evening, once trial is over for the day. Would that be soon enough?'

'No! It won't! That's what I'm trying to tell you! My daughter is insisting, in spite of all my warnings and pleadings, that she is going to go on her own into that courtroom and say whatever comes into her stupid little head. Unless she can talk to that despicable boy's lawyer — you — immediately. In desperation I promised her that somehow I would find you and convince you to come home with me so she can talk directly to you before she makes her mind up about this. I'm hoping you can convince her not to make this silly mistake, Ms. Brevard. I can't see how it would help your case, in any way . . . and I know it would simply ruin her reputation . . . possibly for the rest of her life!' Two large squishy tears forced their way down both sides of her immaculate cheeks, leaving ugly rivulets of black mascara in their wake. Gail was anxious to go with the woman now, knowing that Laura Kincaid was, without a doubt, the girl whose identity Damon Powell was trying to keep a secret. Anna was right. This wouldn't help her case a bit.

'But I *have* to be back at court inside of an hour,'

'Then I'll drive like the wind,' Anna said. 'And the sooner we get started the better.' Gail might still have had reservations about that if she hadn't already caught a glimpse of the perky little red sports car parked at the curb, and Anna was right, she certainly could drive like the wind.

'Laura, this has to be a very short conversation, and there's no time for anything but questions from me and quick answers from you. Is that clear?'

The sullen teenager nodded. Gail was seated on the one clear chair in the girl's well-furnished room with its flat screen TV, computer set-up, books scattered about, a few dolls and keepsakes left over from childhood, and more pants, tops, dresses and their accessories on view in the half-opened closet than Gail had owned in her entire life.

Laura Kincaid may have been close to tears, but they didn't come. She sat rocking back and forth on her bed, but when Gail spoke to her again, she nodded once more. There was some hope, after all, of getting a productive interview out of her in time.

'Do you want your parents to stay in the room while we talk?'

'I suppose so, if I must . . . '

Oliver Kincaid had been glancing longingly at the door, but now turned back and mustered a sickly smile. Anna plopped down on the other side of the bed, murmuring, 'I'm glad we're doing this,' in a voice so low that Gail had to strain to make out the words.

'Laura,' she began. 'I understand from your mother that you wish to testify for Damon Powell in the present trial, and my job, as his attorney, is to determine if *I* think your testimony would be of any help to him.'

Anna Kincaid opened her mouth to speak, but Gail cautioned her with a look.

'Now don't say *anything*, unless I ask you a specific question. And don't answer my questions with more than one sentence. Also, I don't want any of you . . .' she looked meaningfully at Laura's parents, 'to waste my time, and yours, by asking how I might have acquired any information. Is that clear, too?'

'Yes.' All three responded in the affirmative.

'All right, then, let's begin. Are you presently attending school?'

'I recently graduated from high school. I've been accepted and have enrolled in the fall term at Stratton University.'

'And your major is . . . ?'

'I'm not sure. I've started out in Liberal Arts, but I may change that later.'

'Do your teachers consider you to be a good student?'

'Yes — that is, I think so.'

'Now then. Have you ever worked for the Seymour Construction Company?' The Kincaids stirred uncomfortably.

'I — yes. I worked there last summer instead of attending summer school. My parents thought I should have some work experience. I didn't much care for . . . ' She paused at the warning look from Gail.

'And at any time, during your school years, or while you were working during the summer, were you acquainted with — did you 'hang out' with — Vivian Seymour?'

Laura paused a moment. 'Yes. Of course I knew her from school.'

'And what did you think of her? Did you get along with her?'

'She and I were best friends . . . for a while. That is until . . . ' Laura's voice faded away.

'Not to speak ill of the dead, but she was a very domineering girl,' Anna broke in. 'It was Vivian who called all the shots in their group of friends — you know what I'm saying?'

'Please, Mrs. Kincaid. Let Laura respond if you will . . . and you also knew Damon Powell?' This last was directed back to Laura.

'Yes, I knew him.'

'And how well did you know Damon?'

'Well enough.' Laura tossed her head defiantly while Anna bit her lower lip and Oliver bowed his head in embarrassment.

'Are you fond of him?'

'I intend to marry Damon, just as soon as he is free of this ridiculous trial.'

'And how do your parents feel about these intentions? Do they approve of the relationship?'

'They're giving me a hard time about it . . . especially Mother.'

'And so when you and Damon want to get together, you've been forced to meet him in secret so your parents wouldn't know about it, is that correct?'

'Yes. We've been forced to sneak

around like a couple of thieves. All because she . . . '

'And did you sneak out to see him on the night of November fifth? The night Vivian Seymour was murdered?'

'Yes. I did sneak out to see him that night. We were together that night. That's why I'm willing to testify that I know he couldn't have committed this . . . this despicable crime!'

In spite of the tension in the room, Gail had to fight to keep herself from observing dryly that it was a wonder the pair of them hadn't caught colds on such a freezing night.

'And did you suffer a severe nose bleed at that time? And did Damon help you get it stopped?'

'Damon said he didn't mind about that.'

This explained the blood stains found on Damon's clothing. It was, she had to admit, confirmation of a sort. It would be easy enough to prove that the blood didn't belong to Vivian, but if Laura was allowed to testify to all this, then Gail knew her future with the firm would be jeopardized by the Kincaids and their friends. Perhaps she should be grateful that Turner's forensics people had been too lazy to raise the question of the blood-stains on Damon's clothes in the first place. Perhaps this simple truth would not help Damon as much as Laura wished. Perhaps, perhaps . . .

'Tell me, Laura, did Damon give you some kind of keepsake, to seal your relationship with him — to prove that you're his girl?'

'Nothing valuable.'

'He gave you something, though. What was it? Can you show it to us?'

Laura undid the top couple of buttons of her blouse and pulled out the makeshift pendant. 'It was split in half for Damon by a friend. He wears the other half.'

Gail, of course, knew it was physical proof of what Laura had been saying, but it was worthless to her. Damon had already declared his intention to keep the relation-ship a secret and his attorney would be the world's number one idiot if she tried to force him into revealing it.

'Was there any other witness, aside from the two of you, who saw when Damon left you on the night Vivian was killed?'

'He left me just before midnight, but I can't think of any way to prove it. I know no one saw him, besides me, of course.'

'Do you think any of your friends would be willing to testify about the relationship between you and Damon? Were any of them aware of it?'

'I kept quiet about it and I think Damon did too. We didn't really run in the same crowd, so we didn't share the same friends. I doubt if anybody else knew about it.'

'Except for your best friend Vivian perhaps?'

'She had told me that she and Damon had been dating — but that was long before he began seeing me. I don't know if she guessed about us or not. If she did, she didn't say.'

'When did she mention the relationship she had with Damon?'

'I don't remember the day, but it was at the Parkwood Motel. I had gone there to meet friends, and Vivian just happened to be there too.' The Kincaids sat in shocked, open-mouthed disbelief.

None of this, without corroboration, would be of any use to Gail in court, but at least the overall situation had become a little clearer to her — and made more sense now. Damon would not talk about his love for Laura. And she, on the other hand, was itching to shout it from the rooftops. The whole ugly tale would only confirm what everyone believed about Damon — that he was a crude thug who had taken advantage of one young girl — and murdered another in cold blood. No help there.

'Laura, I wish I thought your testimony would be of the slightest help to Damon, but there is absolutely no way, in my most considered opinion, that it would change a thing. If only there was another witness . . . if someone else came forward. Until that happens, I think the best thing you can do for him is to continue to keep your silence.'

Anna Kincaid let out an audible sigh of relief.

'If Merilee Watson's father was Damon's lawyer, like he was supposed to be,' Laura suddenly shouted, 'everything *would* be just fine, because he'd be on TV, and people would just *know* everything there was to know about the whole thing. Merilee, that little idiot, might be laughing at me about it, but I wouldn't care a bit. Not if he was able to get Damon off.'

'Mr. Watson would probably tell you the same thing I am, that your testimony can't possibly save Damon, without a corroborating witness.'

'If no one is going to help Damon,' Laura moaned in teenaged *angst*, 'I might just as well take a handful of sleeping pills and get out of everyone's way!'

Oliver snapped his head around to look at his wife in horror. 'She knows about those pills of yours. I told you.'

'I've hidden them, just to make sure nobody but me has access to them — and I'll hide them again as soon as we're through here.'

'A lot of good that will do . . . '

On the way back to the courthouse, Anna Kincaid thanked Gail for her assistance. 'I think you finally convinced Laura that she couldn't help that — that creature, especially if she insists on making an unholy spectacle of herself.'

'Glad I could help,' Gail said automatically, but she was already giving feverish consideration to the other aspects of the case as she was hurtled toward the next confrontation.

13

'I have read all the papers in the Defense's motion for a D.V.A., a directed verdict of acquittal,' Judge West began. 'In fact, I have read all the papers on both sides of the case.'

Gail waited. Was there some chance, after all, that the judge was going to turn away the flagrant prejudice of these last days and grant her motion?

'The Court will deny the present motion without prejudice or comment.'

So much for last-ditch hopes! Gail nodded, unsurprised.

'Does the Defense wish to make an opening statement at this time?'

'Yes, Your Honor.'

'Proceed.'

'We have spent so much time together here,' Gail began, facing the jury, 'that you must be wondering why I now want to take even more of your time and mine. Certainly you feel that you know most of the important details of this case by now, as well as I do myself. There can't be much more I can offer about what we have already heard. We all know, for instance, that a young local man, Damon Powell, was found in the Long Hills section of Cathcart on the night of November fifth. We know that a gun belonging to his father was found near him, and that that weapon had been fired into the body of a young woman, Vivian Seymour, earlier that night, in the Seymour living room nearby. Three bullets fired from that gun caused the young woman's death. Again, we all know these facts by now.

'What we don't know is: did Damon Powell have any reason to be in the area on that night and, if so, did he perpetrate the crime in question? As the judge will explain to you, the Prosecution must prove to your satisfaction, *beyond a shadow of a doubt*, that Damon Powell went deliberately to Long Hills on the night in question with the preconceived notion of murdering Vivian Seymour. The Defense contends that the Prosecution has not met its burden of proof and, furthermore, will show a valid explanation as to why he was there, that he did not commit the criminal act in question, nor did he have any reason to do so. In other words, he had no *motive* for committing this crime!' Turner, in his seat, grimaced.

'Let me also make it clear that the Defense is *not* required to prove that any other person committed the murder. The Defense does not have the obligation or the resources to say, in so many words, 'Thou art the man!' Judge West will certainly make this clear when he charges you before the start of your collective deliberations on the subject of the guilt or innocence of Damon Powell.' She paused and glanced significantly at West.

'The law,' she went on, 'like journalism and politics, has been taken hostage by our media, and fantasies have been presented, from time to time, about the workings of all three areas of endeavor. But this is not a television show, nor is it reality TV, and the Defense, unlike *Perry Mason*, or the good folks on *Law and*

Order, is not required to produce an alternate solution with pauses for commercial announcements over the next sixty minutes. I am glad to see that the point strikes some of you as amusing. In a way, it certainly is. But that is a very real consideration these days, I think. Large numbers of people seem to have confused real life with outright stories or with stories 'based on' some version of the truth.

'But what we are experiencing here is the real truth! You are the heroes and heroines of this drama, you and you alone will determine the shape of an individual's very real future. Damon Powell won't simply 'disappear' if he is found guilty, and a new dramatic entity won't magically appear to take his place. I ask you to remember that Damon Powell is a very real human being in the throes of a very real and tragic circumstance. I ask you to remember that not only are Vivian Seymour's parents suffering, but Damon's are as well.' She glanced at Nick, sitting near the front of the courtroom.

'All I ask is that you bear all these facts

in mind as you make your deliberations. And I thank you in advance for bearing with me while I make just a very few additional points that seem to me to have the greatest possible importance and bearing on this case.'

* * *

She looked at Judge West and he nodded. 'Very well, Counselor. Call your first witness.'

'The Defense will offer only one witness and calls him now. The Defense calls Damon Powell to the stand.' There was an audible collective gasp as Damon, clean-cut and dapper in his navy blue suit and silk tie, rose and walked swiftly to the stand, looking straight ahead of him. He was the perfect picture of a serious young man anxious to offer his side of the story. So far, so good, she thought as he was sworn in.

'Your name is Damon Powell and you live at 283 Park Drive, is that correct?'

'Yes, ma'am.'

'Please be sure to speak into the

microphone, Damon, so we can all hear you clearly. You were born in Cathcart, are an only child, and still live at home with your parents, is that right?'

He paused. 'My mother had a baby before me, a daughter, but the baby died only a few days after it was born.'

'I'm so sorry. That must have been difficult for your family.' Gail managed to look rueful and just a little surprised, just as if she hadn't suggested to Damon that he mention that fact during his testimony. It might draw a little sympathy for the Powells. It would also appear that he was telling the truth about himself.

'Will you tell us a bit about your education, Damon? Start with the beginning, please, but just mention the highlights.'

'Well, I went to Curtis Elementary, and after that . . . '

'Curtis was originally over on Sixth Street, wasn't it? Wasn't that the school that was rebuilt in a new location about a year ago?' It was a way of bringing out that Damon was a local boy of long standing.

He then spoke briefly about his Middle and High School years, mentioning that his marks had been consistently above what was considered average and that he hadn't caused any major problems while there. He had attended the local junior college for about a year, then had quit and gone to work for his father. He had recently had a change of heart, however, and had gone to the trouble of filling out application papers to Stratton at the end of October, less than a week before Vivian Seymour was killed.

'Why did you change your mind about attending college, Damon?'

'Because of a girl I've been seeing. She keeps telling me I'll never amount to anything without at least a bachelor's degree.'

'Can you tell us more about this girl? Is she somebody you've been seeing steadily?'

'Yes.'

'And have you discussed marriage with her?'

'Yes. I've asked her to marry me.' There was a collective intake of breath in the audience.

'Do the girl's parents approve of your plans?'

'Her parents don't want her to marry me.' Damon looked down. 'And after all this, well, I'm not sure I blame 'em.'

Gail paused just long enough for even the slowest members of the jury to grasp the poignancy of Damon Powell's unrequited love for the unnamed girl.

'Are you prepared at this time to tell us who this girl is, to give us her name?'

'No, ma'am. I won't drag her into this. I just can't. I'm sorry.'

'Thank you, Damon. I understand your concerns. Now we're almost through here.' Gail paused and looked down at her notes, letting the jury have time to reflect on Damon's composure and obvious concern for the reputation and well-being of someone he truly cared about. 'Now, please tell us, in your own words, how you felt and how you were treated by the arresting officers on the night of November fifth, the night Vivian's body was discovered.'

Damon took a long shuddering breath and looked anxiously at Gail, who nodded her encouragement. 'Well, I've already told you about meeting up with my girlfriend. We spent some time together, just . . . well, mostly talking, about our future. She was urging me to go back to school this fall with her this coming fall. She said that, if we did that, went to school, I mean, and tried to stay out of trouble, then she was sure our parents would eventually come around and approve of our engagement. I believed her. I honestly did. But now I'm not sure I even have a future . . . with all that's happened since then.'

'Take your time, Damon. Would you like a glass of water before you continue?'

'No, ma'am. I'm OK. I just want to get this all over with. Get it behind me and try to move on.' He took another deep breath and continued. 'Well, we dozed for awhile. At least, I did. I don't know if she did or not, because when I came to . . . woke up, that is . . . it was time for her to get back to the house, and she urged me to go on home. It was cold out and I guess she didn't want either of us to get sick or something. I don't know . . . ' He hesitated. 'Well, I'll be honest. I was just a little upset at how the evening

241

ended. I felt headachy and grouchy and a little dizzy. Maybe I was coming down with something. I just know something didn't feel right.'

'So after you and your girl talked, you dozed a bit, then woke a while later feeling dizzy and headachy? Had you done any drugs, Damon. Now this is important, so please be honest about this. Did you do any drugs or have anything to drink between the time you and your girl met and the time you left her to return home?'

'No, ma'am. At least I didn't do any drugs. I'll be honest. She had swiped a bottle of booze from her parents' bar . . . but we only had a taste . . . I swear. It was just too cold. To tell you the truth, I was more into just being with her. I probably only took a couple of swallows of the stuff. Then, like I said. I fell asleep.'

'Do you know exactly how long you were asleep? Do you have any idea of the time when you woke up and decided you needed to get home?'

'I can't really say. It didn't seem long. We were cuddling together, all bundled up. I just know I slept for awhile and by the time I woke up she said she had to get back to the house so I'd better get going too.'

'All right. Thank you, Damon for being so honest with us.' Her eyes searched the jury and she thought she saw one or two understanding nods. 'Please continue now. What happened next?'

'Well, I said good night to her and watched her head back toward her house, just to make sure she was OK, you know? Then I decided to take a shortcut I knew of across the Seymour's property, then out to the street. I was taking my time, trying not to fall in the dark, but also thinking about the evening, how it had gone. Like I said, I didn't feel too good, and I was a little upset, mostly at myself, for sleeping when I could have had more time with my girl. As I passed the Seymour house, I looked around a bit. It's a pretty house, and I'd always thought I'd like to end up in a place like that someday. Me and her, you know, in a fancy place like that. I was just sort of standing there, looking at it all, when suddenly these two guys come running up and yelling at me. Well, the one guy, the younger one, was yelling like crazy. The older one was blocking my way out to the street.'

'And what did you do then?'

'I was pretty scared. I didn't know who they were. They just came running up and yelling at me. I thought maybe they were going to mug me . . . or that they might be employees of Mr. Seymour, guards or something like that. Well, I knew I had no business there, but I tried to talk my way out of it by telling them I was just visiting. They weren't buying it, though, and finally I just made a run for it. That was when the younger guy tripped and sprained his ankle, I guess. He was pretty upset about it.'

'Upset? You say the younger officer was upset? How did you know that?'

'He took a punch at me. Right in the stomach. Hurt, too. I don't know why he did that. I hadn't made a move on him. I just wanted to get out of there and go home.'

'One of the Prosecution's major points

is the gun that was found near you. Not only was it identified as the murder weapon, but it has also been identified as belonging to your father. Can you offer any explanation of how the gun got there.'

'I've been thinking a lot about that. You see, in the past, whenever I've walked around some of those areas on my own, I've always been a little nervous about it. Like I said, there's always the possibility of a mugging, and I've been threatened a few times, and a lot of these big estate properties have security guards . . . and they can be pretty scary if they challenge you or get in your face. I know it wasn't a good idea, but I had gotten in the habit of taking my Dad's pistol along whenever I was out on my own like that. It was never my intention to shoot the thing, ever, but I thought if someone tried to threaten me or take me down, at least I could wave it around and maybe scare them off. That's all. I had no intention, ever, of shooting that gun or hurting anyone with it.'

'So you had the gun with you that night? But how did it end up where it was found? And how, in God's name, could it have been used as the murder weapon — if you didn't do it that is?'

'I swear I didn't shoot it that night! Ever! I didn't want that girl dead. I barely knew her. And I have no idea how that gun got where it was found. I don't recall crossing that part of the grounds. And the fact is, I don't recall having the gun after I left my girl.' He gulped in frustration.

'The fact that no powder burns were found on your hands, and no discarded gloves were ever found on or near the scene, would tend to corroborate what you say,' Gail said, then moved on quickly before Turner could object. 'Were you wearing gloves that evening? And if so, do you know what happened to them?'

'No. I didn't have any gloves on at all. And I know I wasn't wearing any earlier. I just don't remember what happened to the gun after I left the house.'

'Thank you, Damon. I only have a few more questions for you now. First, it has been suggested that you were cursing at the time of your arrest. What's more, several witnesses have indicated that you seemed to be angry at the victim, Vivian

Seymour. If you didn't know her very well, why were you so upset with her?'

'It's complicated. You see, one of the reasons I was upset was because my girl told me that Vivian had been spreading rumors about me ... untrue rumors ... but she didn't know whether to believe them or not. When the officers began to take me in, all I could think of was that this was all Vivian's fault ... how things had gone ... how it was ending. I was still feeling a little dizzy, half sick to my stomach ... especially after that guy punched me ... and all I wanted to do was get out of there, go home, and start over. I couldn't figure it all out. Yes, I was upset. Yes, I was cursing. But I truly regret the things I said about Vivian. I just hadn't taken it all in, you see, about her being dead and all. I was just thinking of myself and my own problems, and that was wrong. I see it now.' He took a deep, shuddering breath and the glint of tears in his eyes was visible to everyone in the courtroom.

'Thank you, Damon. You've been very forthcoming. Very honest with us. I know how difficult this has been and I want to thank you for your cooperation. Now the Prosecutor will have a few more questions for you, I'm sure. Please be patient. And please continue to be as honest and forthcoming as you have to this point. Yours,' she said with a nod to Turner then returned to her seat.

'Your Honor,' Turner said, glancing at his watch. 'It's so close to end of our normal day that I'd like to ask the Court's permission to hold off on my cross-examination until we reconvene tomorrow morning. I don't want to make these good people wait for their dinners,' he added, with a smile toward the jury.

'Yes, that seems reasonable,' West consulted his own watch. 'All right. Let's close for today and get back into the cross-examination first thing in the morning.'

'All rise,' the bailiff intoned as West rose and made his way out of the courtroom.

*   *   *

Damon was back on the witness stand at a quarter past ten the next morning. Gail reviewed some of his previous testimony, then again turned to Turner. 'I am through with this stage of the questioning, but I'd like to reserve my right to return to this witness following Mr. Redland's examination.'

'So granted. Mr. Redland?'

'Damon,' Turner smiled at him conspiratorially. 'How well *did* you know Vivian Seymour?'

'Objection, Your Honor. It has already been established that my client knew Miss Seymour only casually. I hardly see the point . . . '

'Denied, Ms. Brevard. You opened this line of questioning yourself. Go ahead, young man, answer the question.'

'I knew her, just to see her around, you know. But I didn't know her well . . . we never dated, for instance . . . and I don't ever recall being alone with her at any time.'

'How did you meet her?'

'Well, I guess my girl actually introduced us . . . just when we ran into her, when we were out, you know.'

'Yes, I know how that might be. You say you were never alone with her at any time? Remember that you're under oath here and we don't want any misunderstanding.' Gail shifted in her seat. 'Do you mean to tell us that you never dated Vivian Seymour?'

'I swear. I never had anything to do with her. Never!'

'And if Vivian had told mutual friends that she was dating you, she was not telling the truth?'

'She was lying, if she ever said such a thing. I don't have a clue why she would lie like that. But she was lying, if she even said it like that.'

'Well then, did she ever make it clear to *you* that she'd have been willing to date you?'

'I already told you. I wasn't around her all that much. I don't recall that we were ever alone together. No, she never told me such a thing.'

Either Damon was a deft liar, or there was enough truth to what he said to make it sound convincing enough.

'And what did your so-called girlfriend say about Vivian Seymour's friendliness toward you?'

'She didn't say anything, 'cause *nothing ever happened*!'

'So you two had never argued about any meetings you might have had with Vivian Seymour?'

'No! I'm telling you! We never argued! Especially about Vivian Seymour!'

'Objection,' Gail rose. 'Badgering the witness.'

'Denied. I'll allow it within reason. Mr. Turner, can we move on?'

Gail glanced at the jury to see how they were reacting to Damon's responses to Turner's grilling. One woman in her late thirties nodded approvingly in Gail's direction, as if to say, 'I told you so!' Gail took a chance and smiled directly at the dark-eyed blonde. It couldn't hurt to have at least one supporter.

'Let me now direct your attention once again to the night of the murder. Please tell the court what you and your girl did on that night.'

'Well, like I said, I went to meet her.'

'And according to your previous testimony, you two had arranged for this meeting?'

'Oh, yeah. Sure.'

'Remind us exactly where the meeting took place?'

'In Long Hills.' Damon was getting impatient. They had been over all this so many times before. Gail kept a watchful eye on him, but decided he was doing well enough to let him work his way through this.

'You met at an agreed-upon place?'

'Yes.'

'What did you do then, the two of you?'

'We went for a walk.'

'And what else did you do, in Long Hills, just before Vivian Seymour was murdered?'

'We talked, a lot, and then we — we hugged and kissed.'

'Wasn't it awfully cold that night? And damp?'

'We had a special spot, on a bench in a gazebo near her house. Yeah, it was cold, but we had our heavy coats and we didn't really feel all that cold . . . I hugged her close to keep her warm.'

Gail had warned him against giving any extra information when he testified, but to talk about protecting his girl friend from the cold was likely to make him more sympathetic.

'And then what?'

'Like I said before. She had to go back home, so I left too.'

'And about what time was that?'

'I honestly don't know. I lost track of time. I don't think we were there very long, but I can't say for sure exactly what time it was.'

'And she just walked away and that was all?'

'Yes.'

'And neither of you had driven to this prearranged meeting?'

'No. She lived close enough to walk, and I like to walk by myself at night, so I hadn't brought a car either.'

'What did you do after she left?'

'I started back toward the street. I felt a little tired and woozy. Just like I said before.' He raised his head and looked defiantly at Turner.

'But after what you agree was a relatively short period of time, you did start to leave the area?'

'Yes. Like I said, it wasn't long — and when I stopped to look at one of the houses from the outside, because it was so pretty, in all the lights you know, the cops jumped me.'

'You're speaking now of the two patrolmen, officers Waghorn and Hudson, who saw you in the vicinity of the Seymour house and gave chase. Why on earth did you run away, if you had done nothing wrong, that is?'

'I honestly don't know. I didn't know who they were at first, and I guess I thought they were attacking me or something. I'll admit I wasn't thinking straight, all right, and I sure didn't want to hang around and argue with them.'

'Now. What about the gun that was found near you?'

'Like I said before, I have no idea how that happened. The last I knew about the gun, it was stashed away in my coat pocket when I left the house. I think now it must have fallen out while I was walking through town up to Long Hills. My real guess is that someone found it and used it to murder Vivian, then threw away the gun when he left the scene. It's the only thing that makes any sense to me.'

'Damon Powell, you've taken an oath to tell the truth, the whole truth, and nothing but the truth, so help you God. With that oath in mind, I ask you now whether on the night of November fifth, following some kind of argument or confrontation, you killed Vivian Seymour in cold blood, then left the scene after disposing of the gun.'

'No! I swear to God I didn't!' He thrust both hands out in front of him with the palms up, perhaps trying to convey his confusion and unhappiness as well as honesty. 'I swear I never went near her on that night.'

'You didn't shoot Vivian Seymour with the gun that was found near you?'

'I swear I didn't.'

'You didn't, in a fit of anger, pull out the gun belonging to your father, one which you have admitted to having with you that night, and maliciously, and with premeditation, shoot Vivian Seymour, leaving her for dead?'

Gail was on her feet, practically screaming at West: 'Objection, Your Honor! This is outrageous! My client has been asked and answered those very same questions a dozen times!'

'Sustained.'

'Then,' Turner continued calmly, 'you swear you are totally and completely innocent of the charges that have been brought against you in this court of law?'

'I'm innocent, I swear to God.'

Gail looked cautiously toward the jury. The dark-eyed blonde juror was nodding encouragingly in Damon's direction. Perhaps there was hope, after all.

West shuffled through a handful of papers on his desk then stated calmly. 'The Court will permit a few more questions from the Prosecution before we are adjourned for the day.'

Turner once again reminded the jury about Damon cursing the dead girl soon after being arrested. And with the memory of that statement fresh in the jury's minds, the courtroom was excused.

14

Turner Redland returned to that very point on the following morning when he resumed his cross-examination.

'Shortly after you were arrested, you cursed the dead girl, didn't you?'

'I don't remember exactly what I said. I've said I was sorry about that.'

'Yes, it must have been upsetting to realize that you'd been caught red-handed by the police right after committing such a ghastly crime.'

'Objection, Your Honor.'

'Sustained. The Special Prosecutor will confine himself to asking questions, not making statements.'

'Yes, Your Honor.' Turner drew a deep breath and whirled on Damon again. 'Were you cursing the dead girl because you had wanted to date her and she very properly refused you?'

'No! I didn't?' Damon swallowed, keeping control — just barely.

'Did you curse her because you had been on drugs that night and you were in a rotten temper because you were coming off some drug?'

'No. I told you. I don't do drugs.'

'You've never taken cocaine?'

'No!'

'What about heroin?'

'No! Never!'

'Marijuana?'

'It's years since I've done any of that!'

'So you *have* used some illegal substance after all? And if you lied about that, it's also possible you're lying about the night you killed Vivian Seymour, too?'

Even as she stood to object, Gail was thinking that she wouldn't have been too surprised to learn that Damon had been on something that particular night. It would help to explain his peculiar behavior, but that wasn't a point she wanted to pursue.

She didn't object because Redland was questioning Damon about matters that hadn't been raised on direct examination, knowing it would make her seem like a nitpicker, and confident by now that

Damon could handle himself in the clinches. What she was most concerned about was establishing a track record, so that if the case ever got to the appeals stage, she would then be allowed to raise those points of law.

West, responding to Gail's *pro forma* objection, sighed, saying to Redland, 'I think, Counselor, that that ground already has been covered.'

'Very well, Your Honor.' Redland, who could only profit from having a guilty verdict brought in, no matter what might happen much later on appeal, seemed satisfied with what he had been able to achieve thus far. Next he asked Damon about the Colt .38 Special that was used against Vivian Seymour. He was working hard to show that Damon had made different statements on the stand than when he had been questioned originally by the police.

'You bought bullets for that gun?'

'Yes. I bought them for my father. He asked me to buy them.'

'Then how did that particular gun get to the crime scene, if not through you? If you didn't drop it there, who did?'

'I have no idea.'

'Well then, do you think your father carried it there. Do you think *he* killed Vivian Seymour?'

'Of course not! Why would he?'

'Why indeed? But you've got no idea how that gun got to where it was found in Long Hills on that night?'

'No. I don't.'

'Your lack of knowledge about how a weapon you were in possession of came to be discarded not far from the scene of a murder is amazing, Mr. Powell, and strains credibility.'

Gail was striving to maintain her self-control and dignity, but that particular remark of Turner's got to her. As hard as she tried, she knew her voice was filled with sarcasm. 'Your Honor, the Special Prosecutor is once again giving us the benefit of his opinions, which the jury must be instructed to ignore during its deliberations.'

'And so is the Defense when a simple objection would serve. I won't warn both sides again in this matter.'

Turner plowed on through the morning and afternoon. Was the intense cross-examination drawing the jury's sympathy to Damon, as she'd hoped? Did they feel ready to take this ordeal and how he handled it into consideration when it came time for them to decide whether Damon would live or die? Would Damon be getting one more chance at life because he was now conducting himself so admirably?

Turner managed to draw a strong reaction from Damon in mid-morning of the next day. 'You claim that you spent the night of the murder in the company of a girl, one of many such girls in your life?'

'She's the *only* girl in my life!' Damon maintained doggedly. 'She's special to me.'

'But weren't all the girls you knew in school special to you as well? What about the dozen or so you must have had contact with during your year in college? Wasn't each one of them special to you, at the time you were with them?'

'No girl was ever as special to me as this one.'

'Special because she doesn't exist, you mean?'

'She exists!'

'Yes, in your head.'

Damon responded angrily. 'I don't get it! First you claim I've been with lots of girls, then when I say I'm seeing a girl now, you say it's all in my head — something I've made up!'

'Look. Maybe you have a dozen girls on the string, and maybe you're hoping to marry the richest of them. I don't know or care about all that. But you claim you went to Long Hills to see one special girl — one whose name you refuse to give us. Isn't it much more likely that you went to Long Hills that night to meet Vivian Seymour, you argued with her, and you ended up by killing her!'

'No!' Damon shouted. 'No! I didn't!'

Gail shot to her feet. 'Your Honor! Please put a stop to this hounding! The witness has been asked this same question, over and over again, and has answered this question many times. Please instruct the Prosecution to phrase his question in the form of a question

— not his own opinion!'

'Sustained. Mr. Redland, you've been warned many times. Please move on with your questioning or I must find you in contempt.'

'Yes, Your Honor. Sorry.' He turned back to Damon. 'All right, if, as you insist, this girl can give you some sort of alibi, where is she? If she loves you so much, why hasn't she come forward under her own volition to testify for you, to help save your life? Why hasn't she?'

That was a shrewd move. Of course Redland's investigators must have told him by now who the girl was and that her parents had objected to her testifying. He also would have deduced that, for whatever reason, Gail did not want her on the stand. But that knowledge did not for one minute deter him from hinting that Damon was lying about her existence.

And just as soon as Turner had made this latest point, the Court, not surprisingly, ordered an adjournment.

★ ★ ★

Gail spent part of her evening with Damon in the visiting room. She needed to warn him that even though the Special Prosecutor had indicated his cross-examination was finished, the ordeal was not over with.

'There'll be at least one redirect, then, following my rebuttal, another recross from him. It's pretty much going to go on until everyone is satisfied they've squeezed you as much as possible.'

Damon looked directly at her. 'But how do you think I've been doing? Up to now, I mean?'

Gail had been wondering since the adjournment how Redland's last question would sit with the jury. That one question, why hadn't Damon's girlfriend come forward to testify, had sounded logical, sensible, and reasonable. And it might very well have made the People's case against her client.

'You're doing great,' Gail said. She knew full well how urgent it was to keep Damon's spirits up. 'You're just fine.'

* * *

Just as Gail predicted, redirect and recross took up the next two full days. Damon, no longer fresh, found it harder and harder to concentrate on the repetitive questions, whether they were asked by Turner or Gail. Several times she was forced to ask for time for her client to recover his composure. Each time he soldiered on, answering each question with consistency, solidly maintaining his innocence, and gaining, she hoped, a grudging admiration from the jury.

* * *

Gail drove back to her own apartment after dinner that night. She had been asked to a farewell party for a colleague, and had grudgingly accepted, although she would much rather have spent the evening going over her final speech to the jury. Sam was a lawyer at the firm with whom she had worked on any number of corporate matters. He was a nice guy who was relocating to California because of his wife's poor health. She hated to see him go, but admired his devotion. Sam spent the entire evening joking about leaving 'all you wage slaves,' but his eyes seemed sad, and he didn't speak with anyone for longer than a minute or two before excusing himself and heading back to the punch bowl.

Most of the partygoers were other corporate lawyers, including three other women who Gail greeted happily. They talked, gossiped, and laughed, and Gail was just beginning to relax a bit when she became aware of Zack Ulrich heading her way.

'What are you doing out with the corporate bunch?' she asked with a grin.

'Oh, I always think of myself as having a foot in both camps,' he said. 'And so do you now, too, it seems.'

'No, Zack, the Powell case is my first criminal matter and my last. So help me!'

'That'd be a shame, missy. You're a natural!'

'But will that be good enough this time?'

'You've got all the right instincts now. And they'll get better, when you're more sure of yourself, Gail. But you've got the brains and will to win. You'll do just fine.'

'I've got an instinct for the jugular — isn't that what you mean?' Gail laughed. 'I'd prefer less instinct and more experience this time around.'

'You're not doing badly, though. Not at all.'

'Are you lulling me into a false sense of security, Zack?'

'Not entirely. But whatever the powers-that-be might have wanted, Gail, you've made a decent showing, I'll give you that much. If this case can be won, you have it in the bag — considering that jurors have a tendency to pay attention only to the matters that interest them — and that they always can be swayed by one or two fanatics . . . '

'Like that vigilante you persuaded me to stick on the jury?' she reminded him.

'Whatever,' he said. 'What I was going to say was that any skilled lawyer has as good a chance as any other of pulling off the wished-for verdict.'

'Zachary,' Gail said, suddenly serious. 'I know you've been hand-in-glove with Turner and his supporters, but tell me again how it's possible I might win this case.'

Just then she spotted Turner Redland working the room like the politician he had become. She watched as he shook hands, laughed, and exchanged pleasantries, all the while obviously calculating who next to approach. She knew the exact second he spotted her. When there was no better connection in sight, he made his way over to her, drink in hand.

'Good to see you, Gail. How're you doing this evening?'

'I'm mad!'

'What a surprise. Aren't you enjoying your maiden voyage into criminal law?'

'The stakes on this particular case are very high — at the same time, the tactics I'm dealing with are pretty low — wouldn't you agree?' Her green eyes challenged him.

Turner was blunt. 'Powell played it a lot dirtier when he killed that poor innocent girl.'

'You seem to forget that Damon hasn't confessed to any of that. No one knows for sure who committed that crime.'

'It certainly looks like he did . . . '

'Appearances can be deceiving . . . I've heard you say so yourself, a thousand times! You're taking it for granted that Damon is the guilty party. There's no excuse for that kind of short-sightedness.'

'That killing was horrible enough to justify any means to obtain justice for the victim's family.'

'You're not hearing me, Turner. Damon is swearing to us that he had a special girlfriend, was with her that night, and, more importantly, he has no idea how Vivian was killed. And that should be enough to persuade the D.A.'s office to leave no stone unturned to get to the truth of the matter.'

'It all may be true, but in my opinion, it's all just a smoke screen. I truly believe he is just making all that up to cover his tracks.'

'But you do admit that you know who the girlfriend is? Damon won't let me subpoena her, but you certainly could, if you had the guts!'

'If . . . and I'm saying only if . . . such a girl actually exists, I doubt that her parents would appreciate you dragging her in to this and sullying her good name. And as far as I'm concerned, that is a lot more important than trying to give that punk some kind of tricked-up alibi.'

'But Turner, I believe she *was* with him that night. And what's more, I think you believe she was, too! You're just afraid to go against the wishes of the upper echelon in this town. I can't believe you've turned into such a coward!'

Turner glared back at her. 'Trust me, Gail. What you want just isn't going to happen. There's no way I'm going to drag some poor kid into court and destroy her reputation on the off chance he's not lying through his teeth.'

'Have you talked to her privately, Turner? Have you done that much?'

'No, I haven't. Nor do I intend to. Whatever she could say to me would only be confirming his lie. She would just be trying to give him an alibi because she fancies herself in love with him — and I'm not going to put her on the stand and allow her to perjure herself. I can't see the point to it.'

'You mean you don't think you could

get some kind of an idea as to whether or not she was telling the truth? Just by talking to her? What harm could that possibly do? Why are you so sure that anyone whose story matches Damon's has got to be lying?'

'Love does strange things to people, as you well know. Just because these two kids swear they were together, it doesn't necessarily follow that she's not lying through her teeth to save him. For all we know, the reason Damon doesn't want her to testify is because he's scared she might get confused and mess up his alibi. Did you ever stop to think of that possibility?'

'But if he *is* innocent, you've all got him between the rock and a hard place,' Gail said. 'I suppose that John West and Floyd Seymour and Oliver Kincaid and the rest of them have decided just how long his sentence will be once you've all made sure he's found guilty. It's despicable!'

Turner flushed in anger, establishing to Gail's satisfaction that her guess was true. 'If Damon Powell didn't kill Vivian

Seymour, he'd have been saved all this trouble. And if you weren't such a bleeding heart, you'd see it that way, too.'

'All I see is that, according to the law, Damon Powell is entitled to the benefit of every doubt. A benefit you, in your collective wisdom, have denied him.'

'Vivian Seymour was entitled to the benefit of every doubt, too, Gail. You're just too stubborn to admit it.'

She turned away from him, sick of the pointless arguing, and certain that they'd only keep repeating what had already been said. As she headed for the door, Turner, a mocking smile planted on his lips, moved ahead of her and once more opened the door and motioned her through in a parody of manners. He had bullied her with that same idiot gesture since their law school days, but it was a lot more grating now.

15

At the end of the third day of recross and redirect examinations, Gail slowly shook her head.

'Nothing more on redirect, Your Honor. I've completed my questioning of the witness.'

'Do you now have any more witnesses?'

'None, and if it please the Court, the Defense rests.'

'Very well. Are you ready to begin your final summary?' When Gail indicated she was prepared, he nodded.

'Your Honor and Ladies and Gentlemen of the Jury,' she said. 'It is now my duty and privilege to summarize for you the case for the Defense. I think we can all agree on the basic purpose of this trial, which is seeking the truth behind the heinous death of a young woman of our community which took place within the sanctity of her own home. However, it is with extreme reluctance and distaste I am now compelled to point out to you that many of the so-called facts which have been presented to you by the Prosecution have been so twisted, and so misrepresented, that very little of what it has told you contains any vestige of the truth at all.'

At least four of the twelve jurors looked up, startled by such a direct statement from Gail, after so many hints she had let fall during the last days of the trial. The dark eyed blonde in particular, nodded vigorously at each of her neighbors in the box, as if to say, once again, '*I told you so!*' Gail had no illusions about the odds of such tacit agreement translating into a vote exonerating her client. Still, if she could manage to stir up some controversy, such discussion amongst the jury members — some small doubts here and there — then there was still hope.

Gail continued with her plan to chip away at the Prosecution's case: 'We have all seen the numerous *leaked*' (she looked pointedly at Turner) 'media accounts strongly hinting that Vivian Seymour was either raped or had consensual sex before her death, stirring up even more sentiment against her murderer — but, amazingly, the Prosecution has provided us with no proof such an outrage actually occurred! No DNA evidence . . . nothing to prove that Vivian Seymour had such a partner just prior to her death. If such proof had been discovered — wouldn't the many forensics specialists who, according to my colleague, 'went over the place with a fine tooth comb,' wouldn't such medical witnesses have been brought in to tell us so?'

Five jurors now nodded, slowly, to be sure, but their expressions all showed varying degrees of reluctant agreement.

'We have heard *ad nauseam* about Damon Powell being drenched in blood from head to foot when he was apprehended in front of the Seymour house and indeed, there *was* some blood on his clothes, but we can assume that that blood did not match that of Vivian Seymour's. Surely the many forensics and medical specialists assigned to this case analyzed the blood from Damon Powell's clothing not long after he was arrested. And once more you can be sure, ladies and gentlemen, if there was any possibility that it *was* Vivian Seymour's blood — again, without any doubt in the world — we would have been informed of that information.

'Yes, witnesses would have been brought to the stand by the dozen, and the Prosecutor himself would have declared it loudly and clearly. And certainly such information would have been made available to the media. But I'm sure I don't need to remind you that *nothing even remotely like that ever took place*! Instead, the Prosecution has been constructing its case like a house of cards. Through half-truths, innuendo, and supposition, and with the collusion of a sensation-hungry media, they've been playing up to the very proper horror any decent citizen of this community would naturally feel about such a terrible crime being committed in its midst. But in its over-zealous attempts to prejudice you the jury against my client in advance, it made a choice to present its evidence in such a way as to blind us all to the real facts in this case.'

Now, with only one exception, the

jurors were giving their undivided attention to Gail's summary. That one exception was Waters, the head of the Law & Order League, who sat with eyes cast stubbornly down and lips pressed tightly in a disapproving frown. Gail wished, not for the first time, that she had kept her own counsel, rather than following Zack's recommendations so blindly. But, onward . . .

'Indeed, ladies and gentlemen of the jury, it is my opinion that the Prosecution has been playing a series of cynical games with you from the very start of this trial, rather than taking part in an enlightened effort to guide us all towards the truth and a just verdict. Again and again, testimony designed to put the defendant in a particularly unflattering light has been timed to be divulged just before a break, so that the 'news' could immediately be broken to the media, and would also be the last item of evidence you might hear before your meal or evening recess. The Prosecution also, falsely in my opinion, claimed it had intentions of calling an adviser of mine as a witness, thus purposely denying the Defense some valuable assistance.'

Gail did not add that she now realized the whole thing had been a ploy designed to get her to accept Zack's advice without question. Advice which she was now certain had been planned deliberately to undermine her client's best interests. How far up did the conspiracy go? she wondered, not for the first time.

'In short, ladies and gentlemen, the Prosecution has been making a mockery of this trial, by shading the truth and spreading innuendo — when not offering outright lies. But the real loser in this game is Damon Powell, whose whole future is at stake here. That's the difference between this game and, say, *Monday Night Football*. This game is being played for keeps. Damon, who in case we have forgotten, is innocent until proven guilty — beyond a shadow of a doubt — and he deserves a fair and impartial trial here. That is his right.

'I will remind you that this awful crime took place in early November, just a few short weeks before Thanksgiving, but here we are, with the trial *coming to a close* just before Christmas. The last time I checked, the Court calendar was just as clogged as ever, but in this one instance, concerning a complicated case involving conflicting scenarios and a perplexing lack of prime evidence, there is almost an indecent rush to judgment. It would seem that the powers to be are in a great haste to sweep this matter up under the rug without the least regard for the defendant's rights.'

Swiftly she next turned her discussion to the body of evidence arrayed against Damon Powell. 'The arresting officers had no reason to apprehend Damon, before he mistook them for assailants and tried to run away. At which time, he was severely beaten for his efforts. All in the name of law and order. Next, his so-called 'mental state' at the time of his arrest has been described in great detail by a consultant who is frequently hired by the police department — even though the said consultant admits he did not have the opportunity to thoroughly examine my client, nor was he asked to do so.'

Damon Powell, she reminded the jury, had never been conclusively connected to the murder weapon. The gun had been fired *three times* into the dead girl's body, but no forensics evidence was ever offered to show that it had been in the possession of Damon Powell at the time of the murder. 'A stranger could have stolen that gun from Damon, or it could have fallen from his pocket and been picked up by someone with an idea to breaking into the Seymour residence. At no time has the Prosecution come forward to show us any evidence of powder burns on Damon's hands or clothing, or any evidence that he was wearing gloves at any time during that night. He had no gloves on him, and none were found at the scene. Once again I must insist, if the Prosecution's forensics specialists had found anything — anything at all to corroborate Damon's connection to the gun believe me, they would have presented such evidence to you.

'Damon Powell himself has told us exactly what happened. Through a pre-arranged date, he met the girl he hopes to marry and spent a short time with her. After meeting her in a deserted hideaway (where a bit of her blood from a nosebleed dripped on his clothing), he fell asleep for a brief time. When he woke, the couple decided to part for the evening, she to return to her home nearby, and he to walk through the Long Hills area to the city street beyond. As he passed the Seymour house, two local police officers spotted him and stopped him for questioning. He panicked and tried to run away, at which point the murder weapon was discovered on the ground. It is difficult to believe that Damon Powell, a reasonably bright young man, would deliberately lead the police to a point where the murder weapon was lying if he indeed was the perpetrator of the crime. Coincidence, yes. Bad luck, certainly. But not the tissue of lies and half-truths such as the Special Prosecutor and his phalanx of investigators have offered here. No, my friends, we are being handed a bright and shiny penny — and they are trying to persuade us that it's big money indeed.

'The choice is yours. You can send

young Damon Powell to prison for as many years as is allowed, for a crime he could not have committed. Or you can set him free to resume finding his own way in the world. The choice is in your hearts and on your consciences, ladies and gentlemen of the jury. May God and common sense be at your side as you make your decisions.'

★   ★   ★

'The Defense has been putting the Prosecution on trial, or trying to, rather than answering the very solid case against Damon Powell,' Turner Redland said at the start of his summary. 'My colleague's reasoning is clever, certainly, as is only to be expected, but every word of it flies in the face of hard common sense.'

Speaking in an easy conversational tone, Turner gave his version of the facts in the case. He took the position of a morally upright man who was being forced to hear a very dirty tale and repeat it to a mixed audience. He offered many everyday examples to explain his points, referring to problems with his car and at another time to differing fees for telephone service. With a word here and a gesture there he seemingly brushed all Gail's reservations away speaking in a condescending, judicial tone. To Gail, his summary was more like the performance of a mid-level actor, than the final argument in a court of law.

★ ★ ★

John West finally began to make his charge and, as did both attorneys in their closing statements, opened with the usual tributes to the jurors for their patience and time. He also carefully doled out measured praise to each of the practitioners who had presented their cases before him.

'Ms. Brevard, indeed,' he noted, 'has never before appeared in a court of criminal law.' And what, Gail wondered, was the jury supposed to make of that?

Finally, the charge was delivered and Gail watched pensively as the jury members were excused to the jury room

283

and their deliberations. One or two looked over at the defense table as they filed out, but the majority left without a glance back. She began to think about what steps might be most effective in case of an appeal. Better to be prepared.

16

She returned to her office for the first time in days and looked over some business for a corporation client. It was good to take her mind off the inevitable. But her thoughts kept drifting to the case at hand. She hoped it wouldn't take too long — unless, of course, a longer deliberation was better for her client.

After freshening up at her hotel, she made her way back to the courthouse an hour or so later, where by chance, it seemed, she ran into Turner heading up the stairs two at a time. His shirt collar was open and he looked relaxed.

He leaned forward to peck Gail's cheek.

'Knock that off!'

'What's the matter, Gail? Still carrying all those hard feelings around?'

'You bet I am, Turner. I'm sick to death of your shenanigans.'

'Didn't you hear? Vengeance is best

served cold.' He paused. 'You know, I actually think a business relationship might work out . . . you've got a lot on the ball. I like the way you operate.'

'Are you serious? In your dreams!'

'I don't see the problem. We're both bright, ambitious . . . we both play to win. That's a good team in the making. Lots of possibilities.'

'I'm sorry, Turner. I just never could get my head around the idea of playing at law like it was some silly game . . . there's just too much at stake.'

'You gotta admit there are similarities, though.' They were nearing the court-room, and, as usual, he fell back to let her go ahead.

'There's only one thing against it, Turner.'

'Name it — and I bet I can change your mind.'

'No, you'll never change my mind about working with a liar and a cheat, Turner. I've got more integrity than that.' And with that she marched ahead and reached out to put her hand on the door.

He laughed and forced his way in front

of her, where once again, to her great disgust, he made the point of holding the door while he motioned her in ahead of him.

'Ladies first!'

★ ★ ★

Once they had been excused, the twelve jurors made their way back down a dark hallway into the claustrophobic jury room where each took a chair at the long narrow table. Several dozen sharpened wooden pencils lay scattered about, along with thick yellow pads of lined paper. Bottled water had been made available for their comfort, as well as tissue boxes. All was ready.

Otto Mayer, leaned back, took a deep breath in relief and said, 'Well, that's over with. Can we send out for coffee and sandwiches now?'

After a brief discussion, the bailiff was dispatched with a hastily put together list of food and drink requirements. While they waited, the jurors stretched, blew their noses, the ladies refreshed their make up and they talked quietly and idly amongst themselves about this and that.

'I really love coffee,' Waters said, smacking his lips in anticipation when the stuff was finally brought in. 'I can't seem to get enough of it.'

'Yeah, but it makes me want to use the — facilities,' Rob Bloch, a young auto mechanic muttered. 'I drink too much of the stuff — pardon me, ladies — and I can't stay out of the — you know?'

Daryl Stoddard, the high school teacher who had been elected foreman in honor of his perceived superior education, decided that was enough chit-chat. He donned his mantle of authority. 'All right, folks. Let's get under way.' There was a general murmur of agreement.

'Just let me finish my Danish,' plump little Ruth Horowitz said, licking her lips and dimpling at quiet young Eugenio Donato, who had made a great point of taking the seat next to her.

Stoddard ignored her. 'Let's take a preliminary ballot. Please write 'Guilty' or 'Not Guilty' on a sheet of paper, fold it in half and pass it along to me. You don't need to sign these.' He took his position seriously and was determined to keep everything on a business-like note.

'We only need to write guilty,' Waters said, glancing around the table. 'Then hand it off to the bailiff and get out of here.'

Stoddard glared at him. 'Let's get started.' As soon as the ballots were turned in he glanced at them then intoned: 'Eleven Guilty, One Not Guilty.'

Waters roared in disbelief. 'I can't believe one of you is stupid enough to think that punk's not guilty!'

Frances Hector cleared her throat. 'Every one of us is entitled to an opinion. You have no right, Mr. Waters, to make such a statement.'

'What does opinion have to do with this? This case was so open-and-shut that a baby in its crib could see he's guilty!'

'I'm not so sure about that,' Fran said, thinking of the old film classic, *The Ox-Bow Incident*. She didn't believe in a rush to judgment.

'What more do you want?' Waters demanded. 'The judge himself thought

Powell was guilty!'

Ruth said thoughtfully, 'Almost a little too much against him, if you ask me. The judge gave me the impression he had made up his own mind too quick.'

Donato shook his head. 'I thought the judge was very fair . . . ' But his voice trailed off as he gazed thoughtfully at the young lady at his side.

The foreman silently called upon a pantheon of deities to bear witness to his agony. 'We have to reach a unanimous verdict,' he said carefully. 'I suggest we speak — one at a time — and please raise your hands to be called. Otherwise, everyone's going to be talking at the same time.'

Mrs. Green disagreed, forcefully. 'We're not students in one of your classrooms, Mr. Stoddard!'

Considerable discussion at cross-purposes erupted. Stoddard continued to hit the table with his pencil, then with a flattened palm, and finally with his fist, all in vain.

Finally the commotion died down a bit, although a few of the jury members continued to whisper fiercely amongst themselves.

'Now just a minute,' Waters said loudly. 'Let's take a vote on whether or not the foreman here has the right to limit discussion. Otherwise, nothing else is gonna get done and we'll be here all night.'

The vote went in favor of the more rational procedure. And since Waters had been instrumental in settling the matter, Stoddard allowed him to open the discussion.

'Look here, I don't want you all to think I'm some kind of stubborn mule. But I can't help agreeing with that government lawyer, the Special Prosecutor, and . . . '

'You *would* agree with him!' Fran sniffed in disgust. It was clear to everyone that she was the lone holdout.

'Please, lady! The Special Prosecutor stated that Powell's father's gun couldn't possibly have been found in Long Hills that night unless Damon Powell brought it there himself. How can you argue with that?'

'Where better to take a gun,' Otto Mayer was picking his words carefully, along with his teeth, 'than to Long Hills, where all the money is?'

'But there's no proof Damon Powell had that in mind,' Fran pointed out in exasperation. 'No one ever suggested such a thing.'

'Well, he was there, wasn't he — and his father's gun was used for the murder.'

'But can we rule out that that was all a coincidence? Absolutely rule it out is what I mean.'

'I suppose it *might* have been a coincidence about the gun, I mean,' Mr. Hauptmann said slowly. He hadn't spoken earlier. 'You can't rule coincidence out — the girl could have been right about that.'

'The lawyer, don't you mean?' Fran said. 'She is a qualified attorney who just happens to be a woman, not a girl.' She had now identified with Gail, and in so doing, had happened upon the one argument with which to bring every woman on the jury over to her side.

Waters did not appreciate the reprimand. 'Let's not make this into one of those 'feminist' issues, please. It's got nothin' to do with this case, not in any way, manner, shape, or form.'

'Hear, hear!' This from Otto Mayer, one of Waters' most fervent allies.

'It seems to me that we're getting away from the point.' Stoddard, fearing he had lost control of the situation, was determined at all costs now to keep the matter of feminism from becoming any part of the deliberations. 'The issue is whether or not Damon Powell committed the murder. That's all we're here to decide.'

'But isn't part of the issue how we perceive the facts in this case?' said Fran, incensed by the exchange and falling back on her vivid recollection of the Henry Fonda film, *Twelve Angry Men*.

'Well I haven't spoken about my own feelings on the matter yet,' said Stoddard. 'Frankly, I can't avoid the conclusion that Powell is guilty of this crime, but I don't think we need to mandate the death penalty here, particularly in view of his youth and no prior criminal record. I suggest we recommend the longest allowable prison sentence instead.'

Waters sniffed. 'He'd probably be out

in six months, given the bleeding hearts who would be crying out about the poor boy's rights. I'm always hearing about people getting long sentences and then being let off before the ink is dry.'

'No! No prison!' Fran interrupted. 'Damon will go crazy in jail. He's just a boy who was meeting his girlfriend and got caught up in this awful thing by mistake. He didn't do anything wrong in the first place — well, not really. Gail was right about everything — all the way down the line.' Her self-identification with the attorney was now complete.

'Let's take another vote — see where we stand,' Stoddard said. He was getting tired of this whole circus.

The ballots were gathered and tallied to reveal that the vote had changed. Eight jurors (all the men) now favored conviction and four (the women) were against.

Waters pounded the table in frustration. 'That Powell kid hated that girl — we know that! And he swore at her, called her terrible names, even after he'd shot her to death with his father's gun! We all know that — Are you all blind!'

Gene Donato gazed wistfully at Ruth Horowitz. 'Maybe there's more to it than that. Maybe we need to talk about it some more.'

Fran addressed herself directly to Waters. 'In other words, Damon Powell thinks all women are just stupid — is that what you're trying to say? Or is that what you believe, Mr. Waters?'

Waters, trying harder than ever to keep control of the situation, snarled back. 'If I was really honest, *Ms.* Hector, I'd ask to put Powell's girlfriend in the electric chair, too!'

The ladies in the room all gasped at his words, but it was Fran who responded. 'I've always wanted to be a lawyer,' she said. 'because I believed it would give me the power to face down all the women-haters out there, just as Gail is trying to do now.'

Stoddard held up a warning hand. He just hoped Waters hadn't pushed the whole thing so far that it would be impossible to herd the women back into line. They'd argue for awhile, he figured, the way women usually did, but hopefully they wouldn't hold out against the on-slaught of facts piled up against Powell. The kid might not have confessed to the crime, but the case against him was sure clear-cut. 'All right, all right, ladies and gentlemen. Let's just see where we are now. Eight of us believe that Damon Powell should be convicted, and four don't. The four ladies, I presume?'

Stony silence confirmed his guess.

Waters persisted with his attack. 'From the moment we got here, Ms. Hector, you've been on the side of that — that woman lawyer — and I, for one, want to know why?'

'Ms. Brevard, you mean? We should give her the respect due her as a lawyer, not just as a woman.' She paused. 'Talking to you is like giving a penny to a blind man. You just can't see what's right before you.'

'What? She said something about a penny. You know, I don't know what you're talking about.' Waters threw up his hands in disgust.

'I wish everyone in this room wasn't so angry about everything,' Mrs. Green said plaintively.

'Angry? Who, me? I'm frustrated because I've been talking until I'm blue in the face about this open-and-shut case. It's as obvious as the noses on your faces. The state has made their case. All the questions have been asked and answered, lawyers have argued and prepared their papers. Plenty of sweat has gone into it, plenty. And at the last minute it's all going to depend on the whim of you four women, one-third of this jury, to make your minds up!'

'I think we're all willing to change our minds, if and when you can prove there's a good reason to do it,' Frances Hector said evenly. 'If you think that boy ought not to have the benefit of every doubt, that the attorney who has worked so hard against such odds, and who is being fought at every turn, is totally wrong then prove it to us.'

The foreman thought he saw a change in two of the women's faces. 'Let's take another ballot.' But when counted, the results were unchanged.

'All you're going on is supposition,' Stoddard said in frustration.

'Are you all forgetting what Gail said about the Special Prosecutor having lied to us. That isn't just a feeling. She said it.'

'Sure, it's a fact she said it, but that doesn't make it true just because she said it.'

'Well, if you have no other facts to present, nothing you say is going to change my mind.' Fran looked around the table, one by one. 'And what's more, I'm pretty sure I'm not the only one who feels that way.'

Gail, if she could have been a mouse in the corner, would scarcely have credited that, after all her painstaking work, the key stumbling block to a verdict against her would rely primarily on the combative attitudes of the jury members.

⋆ ⋆ ⋆

Gail dropped into the small holding cell where her client was waiting tensely with his parents for the verdict. But they were arguing over whether or not Mr. Powell should have testified about the gun and whether their son's defense had been helped or hurt by that omission. Gail left, rather than risk being asked once more to justify her decision to rely instead on a strong summary.

The jury returned after less than two hours — but only to ask for a clarification of the Not Guilty plea. Judge West answered patiently, avoiding the temptation to lecture them, and the panel was locked in for further deliberations.

Once more Gail drove the short distance to her hotel, where she tried to relax as she waited to be notified that a decision had been reached. It had crossed her mind to use this time in getting some work done on her pending cases, but she felt too tired and edgy to do anything except lie down and close her eyes. But sleep eluded her and a few hours later she returned to the courthouse and looked in again on Damon, whose parents had thankfully gone out to grab a bite to eat. He wasn't alone.

The visitor, a flashily-dressed teenager, was a complete stranger to her. Her garish make-up looked too old on her, and the pointy-toed heels were too high for her slight body. She glanced at Gail with interest. 'I watched you in court. I think my father could have done a much better job.'

'It doesn't matter now,' Gail said. 'And who are you — more importantly, what are you doing here?'

'*I'm* Merilee Watson,' she said, as if that explained everything.

And in a way, it did. The name was familiar. Obviously she was the criminal attorney's daughter. Laura Kincaid had mentioned her, too, in unflattering terms.

'How did you get in here?' she demanded.

Merilee pouted her full, red lips. 'My father arranged it. He has connections here, in case you didn't know.'

'I suppose you and Damon have had a nice long talk.' Gail was furious.

'Yes, and it's just beginning to get real interesting.'

Damon was sitting, feet planted together firmly and encased in the shiny black dress shoes Gail had provided for his 'go-to-court' attire. He was staring off into space and seemingly took no notice of the conversation swirling about him. Something else was on his mind and he didn't seem particularly interested in his guest. Most likely, Gail realized, he had been thinking about Laura, and wondering how all this was going to play out.

'You need to wait until Damon is free before you talk to him,' Gail snapped. 'Right now, I need to confer with him, and you need to get out of here.'

Merilee made an exaggerated *moue*, seemingly the only expression of which she was capable. 'Come and see me, Damon, when they let you go. *If* they let you go, that is.' She smiled provocatively, running a pointy tongue over flame-red lips. 'We have a lot more in common than you do with those society girls.'

'Thanks for coming by, Merilee.' Damon seemed in control of his feelings, a social grace he had learned just during the last few weeks, Gail realized, when it had suddenly become such a necessity to his survival.

Merilee clicked out of the room on her too-high heels, hips swaying suggestively. Damon did no more than glance at the provocative sight, then look away.

Gail sighed. In spite of what she had said, there really wasn't much to talk about, but wanting to keep him at ease, she asked, 'What'll you do after this is over?'

'If they let me out of here, you mean?' He shrugged, a long way from the wannabe hoodlum Gail had first met. 'I'll go home, argue with my folks some — maybe go back to college. I'll keep on living . . . surviving.'

Gail realized he had developed at least a nodding acquaintance with the truth over these few last weeks. 'And Laura? What about her?'

'I'm not sure now. I'll keep on dating her — if she wants to. You always think that rich people are cold, but Laura sure isn't.' He didn't seem upset that Laura's name finally had been mentioned aloud between them. He seemed to understand that Gail had known her identity and kept it secret. 'After it's all over, hey, who knows what?'

'You didn't really expect to marry her?'

He smiled, his recent reverie having almost certainly been called to mind.

'Things don't happen quite like that — you know? Not in the real world, only in songs and movies. You take real life, the girl's parents stand in the way, and they can stand real good, too, because they're able to take away the girl's money if she don't do as they say. The girl starts out saying she don't care about nothin' 'cept being with the guy she's crazy about, but she cares. In the real world, she cares, all right.'

He did not sound contemptuous this time. If anything, he seemed to be trying to adjust to the anger within himself and the circumstances his recent trial had made crystal clear to him.

'I'm afraid you just may be right about all that,' Gail said.

Suddenly there were three knocks on the outer door and a uniformed officer entered.

'This is it!'

Gail and Damon looked at each other. Whatever the verdict might be, she didn't think it would be a cause for happiness, or celebration. Anyone who had been this close to a criminal proceeding, who had reluctantly learned just how much of the outcome depended on blind chance, should never be elated, no matter what the verdict. It was an affront to the gods. The only logical response, knowing that coincidence so often played a hand in the game, was to shiver when it was all over and done with — just give a perceptible shiver.

★ ★ ★

'I know there are some points that look like they're in the kid's favor,' Waters had said tiredly. He had made this concession a hundred times, it seemed to him, over the past few hours.

'Well, then, if there's even the slightest doubt, we have to let him go free,' Fran Hector said triumphantly, convinced that her point finally had been made and taken.

'There are still a lot of things against him, facts against him.'

'But we're talking about a human life here. We have to remember that.'

'Two lives,' Waters said. 'Just because

the girl is dead, it doesn't mean that her life isn't important, too.'

'Let's start over from the beginning.' Fran turned over a new page on her pad. Her persistence and energy were making her seem invincible, even to those who didn't agree with her.

'Not again,' Stoddard whispered. 'Please, not again.'

'*If* you don't want to hear it all again,' Miss Horowitz pointed out, 'you know what you have to do.'

'But he's — ' Waters' cheeks turned as red as a beet and he drew a deep breath to calm himself. 'All right, all right, all right! Just to get this miserable travesty over with, I swear I'm now willing to vote not guilty.'

The foreman nodded slowly, a gesture joined by the other members of the jury.

17

Men and women were stirring in the hallway, but not talking. There was a feeling that something serious was happening at last, something that was going to elate one set of relatives and embitter the others. They made room without complaining. The lawyers and a subdued court officer walked through the swinging doors with the tense Damon.

Muffled whispers were soon quieted as the jury members filed in. Most of them, having sat down, looked quizzically over at Damon as if they weren't absolutely certain who he was. One of the women on the jury looked conspiratorially at Gail as if to say in pantomime, *We pulled it off, you and me.*

The judge walked in and settled himself.

Everything moved quickly from then on. The slip with the jury's verdict was brought up silently to the judge, who looked at it and pursed his lips as if he had expected nothing different from them.

The clerk asked the foreman, 'How does the jury find?'

'Not guilty — on all counts.'

A dropped pin could have been heard. No one in the courtroom uttered a word. The silence was all-enveloping, as if it would have been contempt of court to show any reaction.

Richard Yeltoon, in a state of shock, finally rose. 'The People ask that the jury members be polled individually.'

'So ordered.'

Less than a minute passed before the first Not Guilty was spoken and the last. Only Mr. Waters hesitated a split second before confirming his vote.

Gail was holding on to the table to steady herself. An overwhelming flood of weariness had washed over her and she wanted nothing more than to burst into tears of relief, but it was necessary to show confidence and make it clear that she'd never had the slightest doubt about the outcome.

'There will be no demonstrations from the onlookers,' Judge West said somewhat unnecessarily. It had never seriously occurred to him that the verdict would be anything other than the expected 'Guilty on all counts.' 'Damon Powell,' he added. 'You are free and may not be tried upon these charges again. May you prove worthy of the efforts that have been put forward on your behalf. Court is dismissed.'

Pointedly he stood and left without thanking the jury for their work.

Damon's parents rushed forward, his mother embracing and hugging first him and then Gail. A man who resembled the father stood close by, tears running down his face, and it was easy to suppose that Mr. Powell's brother had joined them in support on this day.

'Congratulations, Counselor,' said Turner from behind her as she finally turned from the happy scene and started to leave. His handsome head was tilted forward, and he had forced a smile to his lips. 'The jury really fell for your little-match-girl act, one slender chickie against the forces of government and wealth. A piece of acting no prosecutor could ever have pulled off.'

'Poor Turner,' Gail said, hardly able to hear herself because of a rushing noise inside her ears. She gathered her strength one more time as they reached the door, making a point of reaching ahead to hold it for him, just as he had mockingly done for her so many times before.

Turner Redland opened his lips to say something flecked with anger, but hesitated when he realized there were too many about. He smiled, straightened his shoulders, and walked through the door she held.

18

Gail took a few days off for a visit with Erle and Mother, who agreed, eventually, that Gail had done well enough, even while she still insisted that Joe Norris, Gail's father, would never have agreed to take a criminal case. She spent some quality time with Erle, taking him to a children's film one afternoon, then out for the slurpiest ice cream sundae in town. At the end of her visit she secretly entrusted him with another mesh bag full of shiny pennies, to their mutual delight. 'Take care of your pennies,' she instructed him, 'and one day I'll take you to the bank and show you how to turn them into dollars.'

At the end of her stay, one of her old sorority sisters asked her to fly out to Phoenix to act as a bridesmaid. Gail jumped at the chance to renew old ties, and enjoyed herself immensely through the festivities, until she caught the bride's bouquet by mistake. Turner had been right about one thing, her marriage chances were probably slim to none. Maybe when she was long past the childbearing age she might look for a compatible companion. But she wasn't going to bet the farm . . .

Gail was just placing her offering on the gift table at the reception when she collided with someone behind her.

'Sorry,' she said. 'I think I moved too fast!'

'No harm, no foul,' the man smiled. 'I'm Conrad Osterlitz, by the way — Connie. Bride or groom?'

'Pardon me? Oh, I see. I'm Gail Brevard. Susan was my sorority sister.'

He took her arm and guided her toward the bar where he helped her to champagne and the buffet. It only seemed natural then that they found themselves spending the rest of the evening together. Connie was witty, making her laugh out loud. Then the discussion turned suddenly serious. They seemed to have a great deal in common, and she was even more intrigued to hear that he was a corporate lawyer with a small, but distinguished firm in the Southwest.

'Cathcart, eh?' Connie remarked, helping her to more champagne. 'I have business coming up in Cathcart, sometime in the next week or so if I can get away. I'd like to see you while I'm there . . . if you're free?' He looked at her questioningly.

'Another wedding to attend?'

'Actually, one of my long-time clients wants to make a deal with a guy in Cathcart. The negotiations seem to have hit a snag recently, so I've been delegated to try and work things out.'

'Who's the Cathcart guy?

'Seymour is his name. Floyd Seymour. He's some sort of builder. Have you heard of him?'

Gail grinned. 'Floyd *Armbruster* Seymour is his full name. He's a fat cat in Cathcart. I know him, all right, and I know why he's been out of touch over the past few months. Believe it or not, I think I might have an in with him right now.'

'Hmmm. I know it's a lot to ask of you on such short notice, but I'm sure my guy would be willing to pay quite a bit for a go-between.'

'We'll talk more about it when you get to Cathcart,' Gail said. 'but I'll need to check some things out first.'

'Great! I'll be looking forward to it!'

★ ★ ★

Gail was carrying a letter of resignation when she walked in for her appointment with Judge Morin.

'I hope you know what you're doing, Gail. I suppose you've had a more generous offer from another firm?'

'No. But I refuse to allow myself ever again to be put into the kind of situation where everyone who should be on my side is conspiring against me.'

'You won your case, Gail, so what possible difference can any of that make now?' He didn't even bother to try and deny her charges as he sat back and appraised her over his silver-tipped frames. 'I'm reluctant, for lots of reasons, but I guess I have no choice in the matter, if your mind is made up . . . Do you remember when we threw the big farewell party for Sam Grover?' he said suddenly, almost as an afterthought.

'Of course. I remember it well. It was during the Powell case, when I was just beginning to figure out what was happening.'

'Then I hope you'll let me throw a party for you, Gail. Tomorrow evening. At my house. Just to let you know how much we all think of you.'

'Well, seeing as how it's *my* party, would you invite a few extras? Other than the firm members, I mean. I would particularly like you to invite Turner, Zack — and Judge West.'

'Well, of course, if they're available . . .' His eyes narrowed. 'What do you have in mind, Gail?'

'Just ask them, that's all.'

*   *   *

Gail's mind was made up about her next step. She had begun to make her plans while she was in Phoenix attending her friend's wedding. Meeting Connie had

314

crystallized her ideas, and now everything was falling in to place. Every atom of competitiveness in her, the same spirit which had pushed her into taking on Turner Redland in mock court back at law school and in a real court only recently, was working to force her into gaining one more, very special triumph.

On her way to the party, she made a point of driving slowly past the Seymour Mall, looking it over even more closely than usual. It was all prison-gray concrete, with a pebbled façade. Artificial trees abounded, the real things having been dispatched as too time-consuming. Fountains played merrily on one end where the Great Way, a big box store, was hunkered down, all two blocks of it. And an eight-floor office building hovered midway down the Mall between the Great Way at one end and a bustling Noah's Ark of smaller specialty shops on the other. The parking spaces located at the back of those stores took up about another quarter of the total area. Downtown Cathcart seemed to have been turned into one giant shopping center, she reflected, just in time to lose a goodly portion of its business to the Internet. It probably would continue so long as there were teenagers willing to meet each other there and spend a few bucks on clothes, high-tech gadgets, and the food court, but long-term survival? That might not be as certain as the town prophets once expected. But all that would soon play into her hands.

Right now, the thing she liked best about the Seymour Mall was that it was bringing Connie Osterlitz to Cathcart. A smile played about her lips ever so slightly as she stepped on the gas and sped away toward her new destiny.

* * *

Randolph Morin lived in a charming revamped 1897 carriage house not far from the firm's executive offices and located no more than a stone's throw from the entrance into the Long Hills area.

Gail turned her car over to a valet, and was met at the door by Morin's wife, Kimmie, a smartly-dressed forty-something who prided herself on not having the least interest in her husband's business affairs.

'Hi Gail!' Kimmie warmly embraced Gail, who took a microsecond before hugging her in return. 'Give me your coat and go straight through to the study. Everyone is waiting for you.'

She took her time, meandering down a long entrance hall furnished like a miniature museum, with traditional paintings and antique chests placed tastefully in subtly-lit alcoves. Everything smelled of furniture polish with a sickening overlay of an air freshener she didn't quite recognize. Her clicking heels must have echoed on the hardwood floors, because as soon as she reached them, the double study doors were flung open.

Morin was standing, posed next to a crackling fire on the opposite side of the room, and he smiled easily at her in welcome. His usual silver-rimmed glasses had been abandoned, and he was dressed casually, yet tastefully, in tweeds and cashmere.

'Come in, Gail. Come in. Your friends are waiting.' She had a sudden vision of a fly entering the spider's web.

Easy chairs had been brought in from other rooms and waiters scurried about with trays of drinks and goodies. She looked about, smiling in greeting at the familiar faces.

Judge West was there, seated comfortably, drink in hand, still holding court, she observed, yet obviously enjoying the informal setting.

Zack Ulrich was in attendance too, listening carefully to West's animated discussion, breathing carefully as he always did, in deference to his shaky heart.

Arnie Imlach, the more reserved partner, was gravely inspecting the night view from a window. At the door's closing, he turned just long enough to incline his head courteously in her direction then turned back to the enchanting January snow scene.

Morin finished his cocktail and directed his words to her with a wary heartiness. 'The guests you asked me to invite are here, to congratulate you on your recent success and to wish you continued luck in the future.' His voice lowered. 'Or at least that's why they've been told to come.'

Turner, a few feet away, cocked his handsome head alertly. 'What does that mean — exactly, Judge?'

'Gail has made it very clear that there's a special reason she's asked for us to be called together here tonight.'

'There is, yes,' she agreed, her freshly sun-tanned features suddenly re-arranging themselves for a business discussion. 'Gentlemen, I don't see any reason in beating around the bush. I have a deal I don't think you'll want to refuse.'

★　★　★

'There are a few other points I need to clear up first,' she said, once she had completed outlining the complicated business proposition for the Seymour Mall, which she and Connie had put together. She was sitting at her ease in one of the soft upholstered club chairs scattered about the room.

'You're calling the shots for now,' Arnie said in a jovial manner. 'Just keep in mind that this time isn't billable.'

She waited until the laughter had subsided, sipping at the bracing scotch-and-water Turner had placed in her hand. He, after all, had knowledge of her tastes better than most. His fingers had brushed suggestively against hers, a familiar gesture from the old days, but all she did now was to smile slightly while steadily looking away from him and around the room at the others.

'Now, let's drink to your splendid work on the Powell case,' Zack suggested, forcing himself once again to avert his gaze away from the tempting treats that his precarious health wouldn't allow him to consume. 'You put up a shrewd defense, young lady, keeping Turner here on the run all the way.'

'And doing it in spite of all the trumped-up opposition against me.' Gail raised a hand to forestall all the *pro forma* objections she saw trembling on each man's lips. 'You all believed that Damon Powell had killed the daughter of one of the rich and powerful of Cathcart, and so he *had* to be punished, no matter what the trial might bring out, punished at the very least for having carried on with a girl out of his stratosphere. It's a plot right out of an old *film noir*, all of it.'

'What you're accusing us of is hardly the whole story,' Morin broke in. But the silver fox, for once, was avoiding eye contact with her, and she pressed on.

'Judge, you purposely assigned me to a case that you knew I couldn't possibly win.'

'A rare misjudgment on Randy's part.' Imlach put in unexpectedly, the buttery voice reflecting a certain petulant quality.

'And Zack here attached himself to my case, probably because someone influential asked him to do so,' Gail continued. 'He was right there, to give me bad advice about jury selection and any other matter concerning the trial he could come up with.'

'But you caught on, didn't you?' Zack said. 'I was merely returning a big favor to the guy who asked me to get involved.'

'You weren't doing any favors to me or to Damon Powell, though, were you? Trying to put that young kid away for something he couldn't be proven to have done. And it wasn't any favor to the justice system either, in spite of what you all claim.'

Zack ran an ivory-white hand through his graying hair, looking more uncomfortable at the presence of forbidden food in the room than at her criticism of his professionalism.

'And *you*, Judge West. You ruled against me in court at every opportunity, whether or not I had made some particularly ill-advised motion, and you used your position as a so-called impartial arbiter to make me look as incompetent as possible in front of the jury, over and over again.'

West, still nonchalant, said, 'Well, it certainly worked out well for you, all the same.'

'And still you don't feel badly about what you did, not you — nor anyone else.' Gail paused, her voice breaking ever so slightly, and composed herself again. She refused to cry. Refused to give them even that small satisfaction.

Turner suddenly rose and grabbed another drink from a nearby tray, saying a bit smugly, 'I'm sure I wasn't any help to you, either.'

'*Your* carryings-on didn't strike me as unexpected or out of character, Turner. I will say that much.'

Redland flushed slightly. 'We all thought we were doing what was right, even if it was a little irregular, even if it could be, as you call it, a conspiracy. Our job, as officers of the court in a criminal action, is to see that justice gets done for the community as a whole, not just for the defendant.'

'Of course it is, especially if the defendant is the son of lower-middle-class parents and the victim is the daughter of a rich man, one of the movers and shakers in this city.'

Morin, dropping his professionally florid attitude, met Gail's eyes at last. 'We did what we thought was right, just as Turner says.'

Judge West, annoyed, but wanting to get the grim subject out of the way and go back to socializing, spoke up. 'You have a *mea culpa*, my dear, from each and every one of us.'

Zack Ulrich put in dryly, 'A *mea culpa*

with an explanation, don't you mean?'

'Personally,' Turner Redland said, changing the tenor of the conversation, 'I still think Powell is guilty and so does everybody else here. There just isn't a damn thing we can really do about it now.'

'Too bad.' Now something else was on Gail's mind. 'We've got all that out of the way, so here comes the main deal *I'm* talking about. If I get a satisfactory agreement from Morin and Imlach, I'll be glad to take back my resignation.'

Turner was the one who asked, 'What's the catch? I know you well enough to be sure you want something that won't be easily accomplished.'

Not one pair of eyes was avoiding her. At last she had their undivided attention.

'I'll stay on, instead of exposing Morin and Imlach to all the speculation and gossip about losing one of their stars after the big case they helped load against her. In return, I want to take an occasional case that *isn't* in my usual specialty.'

'You mean other criminal cases.' Imlach had homed in on where she was going with this.

'I know that criminal cases are nerve-wrenching, in ways that most civil cases aren't, and I don't intend to take that many of them, but yes, if the situation is right, I'll want 'em.'

'What's your idea,' Morin finally asked, conceding all, 'of the *right* situation?'

'Any case that looks open-and-shut in favor of the Prosecution.' Gail smiled, almost genuinely, in a way that perhaps only Turner Redland could truly appreciate. 'I want to be able to go into court against the Prosecutor and beat him and his cronies, meaning all of *you* — and keep on beating you in court — again and again!'

19

Vivian Seymour's murderer sprawled comfortably on the floor and gorged on a combination of TV reality shows and buttered popcorn, luxuriating in the knowledge that things had worked out just as planned.

The murder trial itself had been a long drawn-out pleasure that just couldn't be shared with anyone else. The killer had used an innate, if unsuspected, acting ability to play the part of someone who was suffering, somebody whose small universe had been totally shaken up, an individual who was hardly able to find any footing in an insecure world. What a joke!

Take the murder itself. It had been so easy that the killer wouldn't be at all revolted by the thought of going through it all again — and again. The whole idea of planning the killing and later, afterwards, ducking away out of the crosshairs, was thrilling. In a popcorn-tinged reflection, the killer went over each and every cold-blooded detail. What a kick to look back at it all now, knowing that no one else in the world knew, or would ever suspect, just how smart and determined this killer had been.

Vivian Seymour had called to brag about going out, with none other than Damon Powell. It was obvious she planned to rub the killer's nose in it, to laugh about it all among their mutual friends, making the killer-to-be an object of all their coarse jokes and then boasting that it was going to happen again — very soon — perhaps even later that very night!

No wonder then that from the split-second the connection was broken, Vivian Seymour was a dead person. The only regret was that the killing didn't take place any sooner than it did. The killer had always lived on impulse, craving immediate gratification — everything without delay. This time, though, just a tiny delay made all else possible.

Damon showed up at the gazebo, just as they had arranged earlier in the day. It then became merely a matter of giving him a couple of slugs out of the bottle of liquor laced with a handful of sleeping pills. Damon, relaxed from the mixture, went out like a light. It had been like taking candy from a baby then, to remove the loaded pistol out of his inside zippered coat pocket. The idiot had brought the gun on an idle whim, just to swagger a bit and threaten anyone who might challenge his right to be in the Hills. For the killer, however, the gun was an integral part of a scheme Damon knew nothing about, and in which he took no part.

All that needed doing afterwards was to cross the enclave to Vivian's nearby house, talk her way in, all the while crying huge crocodile tears about her so-called 'friend's' treason with Damon. Then, as soon as Viv's back was turned, boom! The deed was done!

Now what the killer craved more than anything else was to make it clear to the whole world that Vivian Seymour had been despicable, and that that fact alone was the cause of her death. The wages of sin, that sort of thing. Vivian had brought on everything that happened to her through her evil actions. The killer was only sorry it was impossible to catch each and every news report or to chat endlessly about it all in every on-line forum. It made the killer feel itchy and restless. Still, mission accomplished, as they say.

Reflecting again on all the delicious moments, the killer especially relished shooting, again and again, into her victim's body. Remembering how easy it had been was enough to make the killer giggle helplessly, nearly choking on the popcorn.

Nothing much more had happened that night. The killer had tossed the gun in the Seymour's yard, returned to the gazebo then cuddled up next to Damon as he slept. He woke a while later in a rotten mood, hung-over from the pill-laced drink and, at the killer's urging, started home. He must have wandered by the Seymour house where he, and the weapon, were discovered by a passing patrol car. The killer hadn't expected that last part, but that detail, if anything, was even more delicious.

Yes, Damon had given good service for a while, and now that he was free it might be possible to use him a few more times. He was a celebrity, after all, and the killer would be the envy of a circle of friends and awe-struck admirers. But still, it was time to make a change. Goodbye, sucker — hello, next victim.

For a brief period during the trial, the killer had yearned to testify, to become the star, the center of attention, someone with whom all of Cathcart would be in sympathy. Damon's lawyer had put an end to that idea, though the impulse quickly ran its course. The temptation to make a dramatic entrance into court, disrupting everything, had faded soon enough.

Damon wouldn't mind being dropped eventually, the killer was sure. After all, he'd get a juicy welcome from that despicable Merilee Watson, so why not? They deserved each other. Despicable. Merilee was despicable . . .

But if Merilee sunk her claws in *before* the killer was done with Damon, Merilee would be poaching, wouldn't she? And it was poaching that had gotten that *despicable* Vivian Seymour just what she deserved.

On reflection, doing away with Merilee, if that became necessary, wouldn't be any more difficult than getting rid of Vivian, which hadn't been hard at all. Best of all, nobody in the whole world, no one in their right mind, actually, would ever connect two such grisly murders to such a sweetheart of a girl — to sweet, innocent-looking Laura Kincaid.

Appearances, after all, could be *so* deceiving!

We do hope that you have enjoyed reading this large print book.

Did you know that all of our titles are available for purchase?

We publish a wide range of high quality large print books including:
Romances, Mysteries, Classics
General Fiction
Non Fiction and Westerns

Special interest titles available in large print are:
The Little Oxford Dictionary
Music Book, Song Book
Hymn Book, Service Book

Also available from us courtesy of Oxford University Press:
Young Readers' Dictionary
(large print edition)
Young Readers' Thesaurus
(large print edition)

For further information or a free brochure, please contact us at:
Ulverscroft Large Print Books Ltd.,
The Green, Bradgate Road, Anstey,
Leicester, LE7 7FU, England.
Tel: (00 44) 0116 236 4325
Fax: (00 44) 0116 234 0205

ONE MURDER AT A TIME

Richard A. Lupoff

They'd been an odd couple, brought together by a murder investigation and discovering that they had an amazing chemistry . . . Hobart Lindsey is a suburban, middle-class, conservative-minded claims adjuster and Marvia Plum is a tough city cop who has fought her way up from the street. But now the couple have split and gone their own ways, both pursuing a series of mysterious crimes. Then fate throws them together again, reuniting them at the scene of a lurid murder . . .

THE 'Q' SQUAD

Gerald Verner

An habitual criminal attempts to snatch Penelope Hayes' handbag, yet is apprehended and charged. Two months later, she's abducted and chloroformed — and again rescued by the police. This time her assailant escapes with her handbag. It seems that the wave of daring criminal gang robberies across London is somehow connected to Penelope's handbag — despite her denials that it contained anything of value. Then she disappears again — and the police have a murder investigation on their hands . . .

MR. BUDD INVESTIGATES

Gerald Verner

Provost Captain Slade Moran arrives from Fort Benson, Colorado, to investigate the disappearance of an army payroll and its military secret. A grim trail has taken him to the empty payroll coach and its murdered escort, with one soldier mysteriously missing. Moran is led to Moundville where he's confronted by desperate men plotting to steal a gold mine. Embroiled in double-cross and mayhem, Moran fears he will fail in his duty. Against all odds, can he succeed?

NEW CASES FOR DOCTOR MORELLE

Ernest Dudley

Young heiress Cynthia Mason lives with her violent stepfather, Samuel Kimber, the controller of her fortune — until she marries. So when she becomes engaged to Peter Lorrimer, she fears Kimber's reaction. Peter, due to call and take her away, talks to Kimber in his study. Meanwhile, Cynthia has tiptoed downstairs and gone — she's vanished without trace. Her friend Miss Frayle, secretary to the criminologist Dr. Morelle, tries to find her — and finds herself a target for murder!

THE EVIL BELOW

Richard A. Lupoff

'*Investigator seeks secretary, amanuensis, and general assistant. Applicant must exhibit courage, strength, willingness to take risks and explore the unknown . . .*' In 1905, John O'Leary had newly arrived in San Francisco. Looking for work, he had answered the advert, little understanding what was required for the post — he'd try anything once. In America he found a world of excitement and danger . . . and working for Abraham ben Zaccheus, San Francisco's most famous psychic detective, there was never a dull moment . . .

A STORM IN A TEACUP

Geraldine Ryan

In the first of four stories of mystery and intrigue, *A Storm in a Teacup*, Kerry has taken over the running of her aunt's café. After quitting her lousy job and equally lousy relationship with Craig, it seemed the perfect antidote. But her chef, with problems of his own, disrupts the smooth running of the café. Then, 'food inspectors' arrive, and vanish with the week's takings. But Kerry remembers something important about the voice of one of the bogus inspectors . . .